GUIDEPOSTS

Older But Wilder

Older But Wilder

(more notes from the pasture)

Effie Leland Wilder

with illustrations by Laurie Allen Klein

CARMEL • NEW YORK 10512

www.guideposts.org

To

My dear fellow "inmates"

at the Presbyterian Home

This Guideposts edition is published by special arrangement with
Peachtree Publishers, Ltd.

Text © 1998 by Effie Leland Wilder
Illustrations © 1998 by Laurie Allen Klein

Jacket illustration by Laurie Allen Klein
Book design by Loraine M. Balcsik
Composition by Dana Celentano

Manufactured in the United States of America

Library of Congress Cataloging-in-Publication Data

Wilder, Effie Leland
    Older but wilder : more notes from the pasture / Effie Leland Wilder; illustrated
    by Laurie Allen Klein. 1st ed.
    p. cm.
    Sequel to: Out to pasture and Over what hill?
    ISBN 1-56145-182-7
    I. Title
    PS3573.I4228044   1998
    813í.54—dc21   98-19371
                                                           CIP

Acknowledgments

Thanks, as usual, to my great editor, Marian Gordin, for her patience and kindness.

For their help and encouragement, I wish to thank George Somers, Jac Chambliss, Sara Cutler, Kathleen Durham, Dan and Jean Sours, Milton Williams, Christine Jordan, Mary Elsie Pow, Bill Boyd, Mary Thrower, Hansell Palme-Reardon, Jim Berry, Harriet Wilders, Martha Waltrip, Nancy Watts, James Osborne, Dr. Alton Brown, Dorothy Walker, Dot Snowden and Mildred Cagle. And to those dear people who gave me stories, and whose names I forgot to write down: please forgive an old lady, and know that I am most grateful.

E. L. W.

About the Name

It is probably not customary to include the author's name in the title of a book that is not strictly about the author, but in this case the temptation was too great. Please bear with the publisher and with me.

E. L. W.

Contents

1

Home Again

August 10th

Here I am back again, Dear Diary, back with you and back at FairAcres Home after too long a time. I have a good reason for the hiatus.

When I had my first knee "transplant" ten years ago I asked the doctor what was the warranty on that piece of metal. "Is it ten years or ten thousand miles?" I asked. He shrugged and said, "Whichever comes first."

Well, sir, I had nine years and eleven and a half months of good service out of that contraption, and then, almost to the day of ten years, the knee began to wiggle and wobble and hurt, *bad.*

The doctor said, "There's nothing to do but to re-tread."

So, two weeks ago I had the pleasure of having my left knee replacement replaced. Two days later, somewhat warily, I asked the doctor again about a guarantee.

"Well, I'll tell you, Miss Hattie," he said, scratching his head, "I'll give you thirty years on the parts, but nothing on the labor." Trust a doctor to protect himself.

He tells me that the state of the art has improved and that the materials have improved. He assures me that this appliance will see me out.

I pray he's right. I would hate to think of a third session in that operating room, even though they joked with me both times under the brilliant lights until a shot of something finally shut my mouth. (My Sam would have had something to say about what it takes to shut my mouth.)

Now if the right knee will just behave itself....

Let's see, thirty years. That's about right. I'll be 105.

August 11th

It's wonderful to be back at The Home again, after a sojourn in two hospitals—one for surgery and one for "rehab," which is short for "Bend that joint till she yells bloody murder." Physical Therapy...PT...Pain and Torture. Those therapists make no concessions to age and white hair. If what they do doesn't hurt like you-know-what, they're not earning their money. One therapist in that gymnasium could have been a drill sergeant in the Marines.

At last I'm in my dear old apartment again, with no nurses bearing down with frightening or embarrassing treatments, no groaning from the other bed, and no rehab. Praise the Lord. (And remember to be thankful, Hattie. Those dedicated therapists got you here with their pain and torture!)

I do have a regimen of exercises to continue. Also, I am equipped with a grand walker for most of my getting around, as well as a wheelchair for use as needed.

August 12th

Christine Summers came to check on me today and caught me up on the latest goings on.

Last week, she recounted, there was a great uproar about a sign that had just been put up very near our gate. Our establishment is situated at the end of a street on the outskirts of the town of Drayton.

It seems that an irate resident came roaring into the lobby one day just before lunch. He was shaking his white head and yelling, "That sign has got to come down *today!*"

Our administrator heard the commotion and came out of his office, and he and everyone else in the vicinity were about to decide that the agitated gentleman was having some kind of seizure. "Those idiots!" the man carried on. "Of all places to put up those two words...."

I wondered what kind of a sign could possibly cause such a fuss, but I understood when Christine explained what the sign said: Dead End.

"Oh, no!" I protested. "But I didn't even notice it when I returned—"

"That's right," she continued. "We *all* joined in the uproar, and Mr. Detwiler called the mayor immediately. The sign was gone before supper!"

She gave me another good laugh with this story.

"I wish you could have been at breakfast this morning,

Hattie. Poor old Susan was flakier than ever. She got up to go after another cup of coffee, and we saw right away that something was wrong. There were two lumps sticking out from her dress, in the back, up high. She had put her bra on backwards!"

"A padded bra," I guessed, giggling.

"Right. She probably turned it around so she could hook it up easier—like I do—and then she forgot to turn it back. It was a *sight*."

"Did anybody say anything?"

"Nobody except Gusta. You know Gusta. She said, 'I declare, Susan, I can't tell whether you're goin' or comin'!'"

August 13th

I lay in bed this morning doing some of my stretching exercises and chuckling over a memory. I suppose nobody can really appreciate it except the people (children, then, mostly) who heard it happen, long summers ago.

It was the week of Vacation Bible School. I had been persuaded to teach a class. I herded my brood to the church. (There were only three children then. Our Extra Dividend had not yet arrived.)

The opening ceremony was to be held in the sanctuary. As we went up the steps to the church's porch we realized that Floppy, our cocker spaniel, had followed us. We shooed him off, we chased him off, we pushed him off, to no avail. He apparently strongly felt the need of some Bible study. It was too late to take him home, so we finally had to let him follow us into the church.

We soon found that Floppy had no intention of repairing to a corner. As we took our seats in a pew, so did he, jumping up beside us happily. All we could do was to hope and pray that he would stay quiet. Maybe we didn't pray hard enough. We were soon treated to a sound that none of us will ever forget.

Our young minister had volunteered to open the week's activities by playing a solo on his trumpet. Now, even a hymn played on a trumpet can fill a large room with large sounds. In this case the blare of the instrument reached new heights when our furry uninvited guest decided to join in.

Floppy turned his head up and back, toward heaven, and howled. Such a howl you've never heard. Ah-*ooooh*. Ah-*oooooooh*. The "ooooh" shook the rafters.

Floppy may have been joining the music in rapture, or he may have been protesting the torment to his ears. I rather think it was the latter. At any rate, the duet went on and on. Neither performer would give way.

My little Nancy was mortified. Her two brothers were convulsed with laughter, as were all the other children. I gave my boys such a look that they had to take action. They grabbed up the dog bodily and hauled him out. To keep him from coming back in, they walked him home, missing the first day of Bible School, which I think did not break their hearts.

I never said anything to the minister about it, nor did he ever mention it to me. When the boys told their father what had happened, Sam said he thought it was "a howling good story."

August 14th

Marcia phoned this afternoon, asking if I would like her to push me in my wheelchair for a ride around the campus. I blessed her and said, "How soon?" I had been feeling so cooped up. I was sitting at the window persisting in those pesky exercises and longing to be outside. It turned out to be one of those days with just a hint of the cooler weather to come, always so welcome in the last weeks of our hot, humid summers.

Marcia gave me a grand ride, and we ended up at the gazebo beside the duck pond, where several residents were enjoying the last hour before our early, early supper. They gave this poor old returned cripple a warm welcome.

When we arrived they were in the midst of teasing Cora because she had just entered another contest. Someone had seen her dropping the telltale envelope in the mailbox.

"Cora's got so many magazines now, there's no place to sit in her room. Every chair is full," said Emily.

"You're right," said Christine. "She's even got magazines on how to raise chickens, and how to make your own furniture."

"Cora," asked Curtis, laughing, "do you think that that Ed McMichael is not rich enough? You're just makin' him richer. That's all you're doin'."

"Now, listen, you-all," protested Cora. "You can tease me all you want to, but I'll tell you something: *Somebody* has to win these contests—and it could just be me! Why not?... And you-all had better hope it *is* me, because if I win I'm

Floppy turned his head up and back,
toward heaven, and howled.

going to put up a building here at The Home with a swimming pool in it. A *big* one."

That caused some comment. Many people here have wanted a pool. It would be wonderful for physical therapy. Last year, a committee of residents had even approached the Powers That Be—the corporation that owns FairAcres—but were told that a building and a pool would be too costly. The only way they could do it would be to raise our monthly maintenance fees—again. Goodness knows we don't want that.

The talk turned to other contests, and got around to the Georgia lottery. Curtis said, "I reckon I waste too much money buyin' those tickets, but a fellow in Columbia won a pile last year, and—"

"And didn't a woman in Rock Hill win a million dollars?" asked Hugh. "On just one ticket? She added up her kids' ages to get the number—or something crazy like that. It's a cryin' shame, the money that goes to that Georgia racket from South Carolina. We ought to have a racket of our own. We could have better schools."

They talked about sweepstakes for a while, and then Curtis said, "By the way, Paul, I heard about a contest to come up with a name. That ought to interest you. Weren't you in the advertising business?"

"Right. And I like to name things."

"Have you heard about the National Motors contest?" Paul shook his head.

"Well, sir, they're bringing out a new car this year, for their sixtieth anniversary, and they want a name for it."

"What kind of car?"

"A fancy sedan, I think. There's a grand prize of, I believe, $100,000!"

Paul raised his eyebrows. "That's interesting," he said, "and right up my alley. I used to have some automobile dealer accounts."

"Tell you what, Paul," said Hugh. "You put your mind to it, and we'll all help you. I always thought a good name for a car would be Sweet Chariot."

That got a laugh. Somebody sang a bar or two of "Swing Low."

Curtis said, "I've got a better one." He put his mouth to Paul's ear. I wasn't supposed to hear, but I did. (My eavesdropping genes are working well, as usual.) "Instead of a Coupe de Ville, you could call it Poop de Ville." Curtis nearly fell out of his chair, laughing at his own wit.

I knew I was home again.

2

Good Humor Men

August 17th

I'll swear to it. I found it in the Bible:
> Strengthen ye the weak hands,
> and confirm the feeble knees.

I want to put exclamation points after that verse. It's in the thirty-fifth chapter of Isaiah.

Well, something is "confirming" my feeble knee. I've been using one of the new fancy walkers—the kind with three wheels—the Cadillac of walkers. They're great: light and flexible. But today I graduated to a cane and marched into the dining room, real proud of myself. My tablemates looked beautiful to me. The meatloaf, mashed potatoes, vegetables, and tea tasted like ambrosia and nectar.

Somebody at the table pointed to poor old Theodora— we call her Theo—who had stopped in front of the large goldfish tank, just inside the dining room. We could see her mouth moving. She talks to the fish every day. She has given them names and she calls them to her and confides in them. She has made it plain to us that she thinks we're a pretty sorry lot. We wondered what she was telling her piscine friends about us today.

Somebody saw Virginia take a dear little enameled pill box out of her bag and remarked on the beauty of it. "Yes, isn't it lovely?" she said, with a twinkle in her eye. "I keep only my best pills in here." We joined in her merry chuckle.

It is a blessing to be around the table with friends again. And I told them how much I appreciate their kindness and their ready laughter, especially about the foibles of growing older. Hugh added his endorsement of humor, recounting, "Our minister told us that he always tries to lead into his sermons with a little humor. I told him, 'Good! A little bit of sugar helps the medicine go down.'"

August 18th

I went into the library after supper tonight and took my magazine over to a chair by a slightly open window. I hoped that Paul and Curtis would go out on the terrace to smoke. (No smoking is allowed in our buildings.) I love to hear their ruminations and their funny stories.

Sure enough, they went out and lit up.

Paul said, "Curtis, you surely are looking better these days. Have you got that prostate trouble licked?"

Curtis chuckled. "Maybe not licked, but discouraged right good. That doctor really knows his stuff. And something else he knows is how to charge. Oh, man! If Uncle Sam wasn't picking up most of the bill, I'd be sunk."

"I know what you mean. My doctor put a new wing on his house after my surgery, three years ago. And the hospital! Five dollars for a Band-Aid was regulation."

They were quiet for a minute or two, and then Curtis said, "I remember the old days, when a doctor would go out to a farmhouse and deliver a baby, knowing that he might be paid in produce. Try to get one to do that now!"

"Well," interjected Paul, "an honest-to-goodness home-grown tomato would be worth something to *me* these days."

"I know what you mean—one that actually tastes like a tomato, not like those sorry excuses for tomatoes they try to pass off in the supermarket. But, oh, doctors today: they want to see that insurance card before they'll even look at you. I tell you, Paul, there're too many changes…. But, if I start worryin' about 'em I can't sleep…. I just leave it all in the lap of the gods…. You ever wonder about that lap?"

"No, but it must be a pretty big lap, for all we leave in it…. Hey, I heard a good story yesterday. An old lady of a hundred and two was visited by a young reporter who inquired as to the cause of her longevity.

"'It's because I've been happy. Happy all my life,' she told him.

"'Has your health been good?' he asked.

"'Superb!' she answered.

"'Well'—he hesitated—'have you ever been bedridden?'

"'Oh, yes,' she said. 'Many, many times…and twice in a buggy!'"

Curtis whooped. I could hear him slapping his thigh. They smoked quietly for a while, and then Curtis said, "Now I'll tell you one. An eighty-six-year-old man went to his doctor. He said he had married a twenty-two-year-old girl, and he was having a problem.

"'I'm not surprised,' said the doctor, chuckling. 'Tell me about it.'

"'Well,' said the old fellow, 'here's my trouble, Doc. I jest can't remember her name!'"

My shoulders shook. Those two are priceless. I hope they wouldn't mind my listening, if they knew. Somehow I don't think they would begrudge me the pleasure.

Curtis said, "Are you thinkin' about car names?"

"I surely am. What d'you think about Felicity?"

"I don't know," said Curtis, after a moment. "No offense, but that sounds kind of sissified to me."

Paul laughed. "I guess you're right. How about Unity? Or Condor? Or have they named one that already?"

"I don't think so. Condor. That sounds good to me. A big, strong bird.... I thought of one. How about Harmony?"

"I like that," said Paul.

"The only thing is," said Curtis, "down here they'd probably call it Hominy! And then it would get down to Grits."

We all ended the day in high good humor.

August 19th

Sidney and Retta Metcalf are now living in a brick cottage on the campus—the largest one, with two bedrooms and a nice garden. They are "giving the lie" to people who

said they were too old when their courtship and marriage
shook up this place last year. It does me good to see how
contented they are together.

Retta came to see me today and brought with her two
lovely yellow squash from their "crop." She wanted to talk
about some upcoming events. The Home plans to take us
in the big bus to the zoo in Columbia. We often take
advantage of such outings. Sidney has given up driving
because of his poor vision, and though Retta and I still drive
some, we are always happy to have transportation provided.

I told her about a conversation I overheard in my rehab
class that provided another good reason for us not to be
burdened with taking our own cars.

> *First gentleman:* I'm driving down to the Coliseum
> in Charleston tonight for the big doin's, but I'm worried.
> When we come out after the show, I'll have a hard time
> finding my car. They all look alike in the dark.
>
> *Second gentleman:* I'll tell you what I've learned to
> do. I know the general area where I parked, and when
> I get there I start clicking the "opener" on my new car
> key—the thing that opens my car doors and trunk. I
> keep pressing that button, and when a trunk pops up,
> I know that's my car!

We couldn't imagine doing that ourselves, but we had to
admit that it was a right smart idea.

Retta also mentioned going to Charleston to see a New
York company in a revival of *Life with Father.*

"I feel sure Sidney will want to see that play," said Retta. "Did you know that he played in amateur theatricals when he was young? He did—in college and in the Little Theater in his hometown. I'll bet he was wonderful.... He told me about a funny thing that happened when he was at the university. Maybe you can use this in your next book, Hattie.

"He said he took part in a production of *A Midsummer Night's Dream* with the college players, and the next day he was walking down the street when he met a group of his friends—boys and girls. One of the girls called out, 'Oh, Sidney! I *loved* your Bottom last night!' He said it took him a long time to live that down, and he never wanted to play the part of Bottom again!"

August 20th

When I came out of the dining room after lunch today, Arthur Priest was waiting for me.

"Could we talk a minute, Miss Hattie?"

"Of course, Arthur." I'm always glad to talk to this smart and personable young man, so valuable in our Maintenance Department.

"Let's go out to that new bench in the Butterfly Garden," he suggested.

We talked a minute about his fetching little family. Then he said, "There's something happening that I thought you might want to know about. Something good, I hope."

He told me that he had heard some of the residents talking about missing their own home gardens and the fresh vegetables from them.

"They're right," I said. "Just about everything they serve here is canned or frozen. I got such pleasure from the fresh crookneck squash Mrs. Metcalf brought me from her little cottage garden!"

Arthur continued. "I was raised on a farm. Always had plenty of good, fresh food to eat. Helped to grow it, too…. Anyway, I couldn't get the matter off my mind, and I finally went to Mr. Detwiler with this idea: There's a kind of a cleared place on my property, behind the house. I'm sure somebody had a garden there once, a big one, more than half an acre. I told Mr. D. that next year I could grow beans and corn and cabbages and okra and tomatoes there, working after hours and on Saturdays. Dolly and I and the boys will have plenty, with enough left over to sell to The Home for less than what the canned and frozen stuff is costing—and I could still make a little money on the deal. He talked to the chef about it, and they want me to start planning and get the ground ready this fall. Mr. Detwiler even offered the use of one of The Home's tractors! I thought maybe you would want to tell the people about it."

"I'll shout it to them, Arthur! Maybe I'll put a little article about the good news in *Family Affairs*…. I could call it 'Fresh Kabbages from Kudzu Kottage!' It's a wonderful idea. Maybe some of us could help you a little—there's many a farm-raised youngster inside these elderly bodies," I said, laughing.

"Yes, ma'am. And you can help Chef Carter snap the beans and shuck the corn."

"That we will, gladly!" I said, tickled to death at the prospect. Visions danced in my head—not of sugarplums but

of fresh baby lima beans and plump, juicy kernels of Silver
Queen corn.

Really, when all is said and done, it takes so little to keep
us happy!

I couldn't resist repeating to Arthur a story about one of
the other fellows on the staff. Mary recounted the episode
recently. "I think his name is Cory," she told us. "When he
came down the hall, he must have been feeling extra good,
because he called out, 'Good mornin', Sweetie!' To which I
replied, '*Miss* Sweetie, to you!'"

August 21st

I have found it to be a law of nature: If you drop something, it is going to roll twice as far as you thought it would,
and in an unexpected direction.

This morning I was sitting in my rocking chair, watching
the news on TV and putting on my gold earrings. One
dropped. There was only so much space it could have fallen
in. Or at least that's what I *thought*. I searched until I was
dizzy, and gave up. Later today I saw it shining up at me
(quite sassily, it seemed) from under the edge of a table
across the room. Inanimate objects can be so perverse.

Remarks I heard at the table today:

"Brussels sprouts are so cute. I just wish they tasted good."
(I'll have to advise Arthur against giving space to that par-
ticular crop.)

"Don't tell that Tinken woman anything. She's pro-
grammed to transmit, not to receive."

Poor Geneva Tinken. So much of life upsets and defeats

her. She insists on calling our beauty shop the "beauty saloon." I don't know why she makes appointments and keeps them, because she never likes what the operators do to her. People in rooms near hers say that she goes home and undoes the hairdo completely, raking the comb viciously through her locks and muttering about the "crazy operators in that crazy saloon." Once she said, "They must've taken a vow to see how bad they can make me look."

I differ with her completely about our two beauticians. I think they are long-suffering saints. They not only have to put up with old ladies who miss appointments or get the hours mixed up or forget to bring any money, but also have to listen politely to our endless chattering about old days and old ways while they try to find a way to hide large ears or hearing aids with thinning hair, and to fix a hairdo that will cover bald spots and places where the pink scalp shows through the ever-receding tresses.

Hooray for the Beauty Saloon!

August 22nd

Today Lucille, our Program Director at The Home, asked several of us if we would be pen pals with children in a third-grade class at a Drayton school. She is a friend of their teacher, Mrs. Trotter. School will be starting next week, and Mrs. Trotter thought it would be good for the children to correspond with older people. Several of us agreed to take part.

It seems so strange for school to be starting this early. It was always well after Labor Day when we went back to class.

I remember when education had to revolve around the schedule of children working on family farms. School couldn't start until after the crops were harvested. Another way that times have changed!

August 25th

Someone asked Ethel, "Why don't you bake some cookies once in a while, Ethel?"

"Me? Bake cookies? I didn't come to a retirement home to *cook*."

"But you've got a nice oven in your kitchenette, and it's just going to waste."

"It's not going to waste. I've got about fifteen pairs of shoes in that oven! The closets are so darn *small....*"

When the laughter died down, Louly said, "I went to see a friend who lives at the Methodist Home, and guess what she had done in her kitchen? She'd taken the tops off of the four burners on her stove and put potted plants in those holes! They looked real pretty, she said, and she had the nicest smelling kitchen in the whole place!"

August 28th

I was doing a bit of reorganizing today. I haven't become so desperate for room that I have to put shoes in the oven, but I did have to clear out some space. It put me in a versifying mood, and I came up with two rhymes.

MULTIPLICATION

I cleaned my closet today and found
Forty bare coat hangers hanging around.
There were only twenty a week ago,
So here is what I want to know:
(Someone, please, my query heed)
Do hangers in dark closets *breed*?

A CLOSET'S CONSPIRACY

Time to get out last year's clothes.
Why are they tighter? Goodness knows.
Every year this thought I've thunk:
I *can't* be bigger. They *must* have shrunk!

3

Treasures

September 2nd

Just back from a few days at the beach with children, grands, and my only great-grand. It was wonderful—except when I got in the bathtub and found there was no way to hoist myself out; no rubber mat, no bar, no rod—nothing to hold on to. Getting in wasn't so bad, but getting out, wet and slippery, was downright dangerous. I slid and foundered and thought I would have to yell for somebody to call the Coast Guard to come and get the Poor Old Soul out of the tub. I finally managed it by performing contortions. There was rejoicing. Grandmother was clean and unbroken. I vowed to take sponge baths the rest of the time.

The conglomeration of cars parked at the beach house was something to see. Two of them were so low-slung that

I'd practically have to kneel down to get in them, while the vans were so high I needed a ladder. Such extremes.

Sam would have been proud of the acuity and ingenuity of his grandchildren. I noticed, on this vacation, that nothing daunts them—not traffic or gadgetry or Instructions-on-the-Back, or the myriad complications of this tumultuous age. Were he and I ever that self-assured?

How good it is to be home again, to my good bed, my un-sandy sheets, my strong reading light, my bars to pull up by, my feel-good chair, and my very own refrigerator where I know there will always be a Classic Coke and not just a collection of weird "sodas"—and where there isn't an endless and wild wind blowing with the main purpose of making a hooraw's nest out of my hair. Gray hair is bad enough. Wind-blown gray hair is witchy-fied.

Later

One morning when I was at the beach, I woke up early enough to see the sun rise. From the screened porch I had a prime view, all to myself. I didn't see another human soul watching. Two dark birds lit on the railing of the pier in front of the house. They and I faced the east, and waited.

Emily Dickinson wrote that the sun rises "a ribbon at a time," and that's exactly what happened that morning. Rosy hues began to streak the blue of the eastern horizon. White cotton-ball clouds turned a dainty pink. The gently rolling surf was the only sound to accompany the rise of the great orb over the platinum sea. It came up strong and golden.

A number of adjectives sprang to mind: awesome, brilliant, overpowering—and another—comforting. God and Old Sol were giving us another day to play with.

Still later

I hear so many older people say, "I just do that to pass the time." To pass the time. Hmmmmm. Time is passing for me too fast. I want to hold on to it. I want to grab it and say, Wait! Wait! There's still so much I haven't done. So much I want to do again, vicariously—to do and see and taste and feel and experience—even if I must do most of it now through books and movies and television. I can sit in comfort and get a thrill from a printed page (in large print) or a 19-inch screen. With my old bones ensconced in a soft padded chair I can go with James Hilton to the top of Tibet; I can see the way they dressed and danced and flirted in the time of Jane Austen's ladies; I can listen to William Buckley's erudite sentences and be pleased when his eyes sparkle over a point he has made; I can get a thrill hearing the bat meet the ball for a home run in a close game; I can be uplifted by a televised sermon.

I am thankful for the great ways to fill the hours that are left to me.

Television has truly metamorphosed old age. I remember visiting country relatives as a child. In the evenings there wasn't much to do but sit on the front porch and watch the bullbats flit around, which gets tiresome fast. There were books, but not enough light from the oil lamps to read by in any comfort. Before long I'd hear the old folks yawning with boredom. Finally they'd give up and go to bed, around half-past eight.

One morning when I was at the beach,
I woke up early enough to see the sun rise.

Good gracious! At half-past eight these nights I'm all a-twitter, trying to decide which show on which channel will be the best to watch. If there are two good ones, maybe I will switch back and forth and get a good taste of both!

I am pleased when riding through the country these days to see a television antenna atop every house or a satellite dish in the yard. Even if they're just watching a rerun of *Seinfeld* at night, he's better than the bullbats!

September 5th

I just returned from my walk, where I saw a wondrous *thing*. There in the evening sky a plane had left a contrail. I watched as it broke up and feathered, shiny white against a cerulean sky. *Beau*tiful. There was a pale new moon rising. The contrail covered it, then uncovered it and sailed on toward Beaufort and Savannah. I hope a lot of people down that way are looking.

I'm so glad I live in a place where I can get to see an expanse of sky, especially when limbs and needles and cones of tall, graceful pine trees are silhouetted against it. Nothing could be more satisfying to old eyes.

I ran into Christine who spent Labor Day weekend in Atlanta, where she had gone to attend her great-niece's wedding. She came back with a good, true story, one that pleased me, in this time of fly-by-night marriages.

Her great-nephew, nineteen years old, had to be the one to escort his sister down the aisle and give her away, since the father had died. On the day of the wedding somebody heard him say to the groom, "Now my friend, when I give

my sister to you tonight I want you to know one thing, and
know it good: This is not a Wal-Mart deal. There will be no
receipt for returning or exchanging."

Good for him! Maybe this couple will decide to be satis-
fied with their "purchase."

September 6th

I have enjoyed getting letters from my new third-grade
pen pal, a little girl named Amanda Pate. She is completely
uninhibited, which makes her letters fresh and welcome.

Here is her first letter:

> Dear Mrs. McNair,
>   I got your letter today. It was nice. I like the
> third grade. We are not babys any more. My
> last baby tooth came out yesterday. Mrs.
> Trotter wrapped it up for me to take home.
> Last night I put it under my pillow and gess
> what? This morning that napkin had a quater
> in it, the last quater I will get from a tooth.
> Did you have a Tooth Fairy when you were
> little?
>   Please write to me soon.
>   Love,
>   Amanda

I was a little startled at something she wrote in her second letter, which I received today. She said she was glad to
get my letter, and liked hearing about our ducks and about
our chimes (the ones that play hymns from our chapel's

steeple), and then she said, "Excuse me, Mrs. McNair, but could you please print, like I do?" Oh, my! She couldn't read my writing!

I had to write her back this afternoon and say, "I'm very sorry, Amanda, but if I tried to print, you really couldn't make it out. I was never taught to print. We went into cursive writing in the first grade. I will try to write plainer."

September 7th

I was visiting with our guest minister after the service today and was late getting to the dining room. "Hattie," Phoebe said as I sat down, "we were talking about the treasures that people find sometimes in attics and old trunks and things. Not so much these days as in the 'olden days.' Not many attics any more. Not even many trunks." Phoebe's a fairly new resident, having moved into one of the cottages in June.

Virginia suddenly blurted out. "That reminds me. I've got a note from General Lee. At least, I *think* I've still got it."

Seven pairs of eyes focused on Virginia. All chewing stopped.

"You *think* you've still got it?" someone asked. "Don't you *know?*"

"A note from General Lee? As in Robert *Edward* Lee?" Bill Nixon sounded unbelieving.

Virginia gets easily flustered these days. She's feeling her eighty-three years. "Well," she said, "I had it before I moved here. All my brothers and sisters are gone, so it fell to me. I think it's still in my desk.... It's not a real letter. It's a note on the back of a circular about his college. What was the college he went to as president, after the war?"

"Washington College," I said. "The name was later changed to Washington and Lee."

"Who did he write the note to, Virginia?" somebody asked.

"I think my daddy told me that his father wrote to the general to get some information about the college. He was thinking about sending his oldest son—my father's older brother, George—there to college."

"Did he?"

"No. I suppose the fee—something like seventy-five dollars a session—was too high. This was right after the war, and my grandfather, who had been a major in the Confederate army, had lost all his property to carpetbaggers."

I shook my head in sorrow. It kills me to think about what people down here went through after that war, The War.

I had to hold myself in check. I knew they didn't want a tirade from me right then. Our minds were on that note. Several of us made a date to go to Virginia's room that afternoon about four o'clock. "I'll try to find it before then," she said.

When we arrived, she was waving something proudly. "I found it in the bottom drawer of my desk!" she announced.

She held up the folded circular. There was no envelope. I suppose somewhere along the way someone had taken that for the stamp. The paper was worn thin in two places where it had been folded for well over a hundred years. I held my breath. I was so afraid she would tear it.

First we looked at the note on the back. The handwriting was faded but beautiful. It was headed Lexington, Va., May 4th, 1866, and it said:

My dear Sir:
Your letter of the 23rd ult. is just in, and in reply I send a printed circular with all the information you desire.
Thanking you for your kind wishes, and trusting you may experience every happiness,
I am very truly yours,
R. E. Lee

Bill Nixon touched the signature with his fingertips. A Virginian and a graduate of the Virginia Military Institute, he has a true Southerner's reverence for the great general.

We studied the printed circular with a magnifying glass. Five professors were listed, including the general himself, who taught Mental and Moral Science. Freshman and sophomore classes studied only Latin, Greek, and Mathematics. Physical Science and Philosophy were added in the last two years.

Applicants for admission to the freshman class must have read at least four books of Caesar. There was no mention of English in the curriculum. There was a statement saying they hoped to teach French sometime in the future. The fee was $75 a session, with board and room another $25.

Maybe because there were so few young men left in Virginia, the school seemed anxious to recruit students. A line said: "A student may enter at any time of the year."

"What are you going to do with this, Virginia?" Bill asked.
"I don't know. What do you think I should do?"

"Well, first of all I think it should be framed in a special way, with glass on both sides, so that both the circular and the note can be seen. Then...what about giving it to the Museum of the Confederacy in Richmond, where it could be preserved and where a lot of people could see it?" He glanced around at the rest of us. "What do you-all think?"

We all nodded. Phoebe said, "They would undoubtedly give her a receipt that would allow her to take a deduction on her tax return." Phoebe is so sensible.

So—that's what Virginia has decided to do. She plans to contact the museum by letter this week. I think it's good of her to part with a family heirloom. Much better that than to have it go to pieces in a desk drawer.

I wonder if there are any other such treasures hidden away at this place? Any other valuable, nostalgic memorabilia of days long gone?

September 8th

In a gathering today we were talking about the Computer Age, about the new ways of doing business, even over the telephone.

Louly said, "I have to call the main office of my bank in Columbia every now and then to see if my balance is right."

(I happen to know that she doesn't *have* a balance; doesn't bother to add her checks—just puts down whatever the bank tells her over the phone.)

"I have their free long-distance phone number written

on my checkbook," continued Louly. "I dial it. In a minute
I hear, 'If you have a touch phone, press so-and-so; if you
have a dial phone, do so-and-so; if you are calling from so-
and-so....' Anyway, I don't do a thing. I don't press anything. I just wait, and after a while they give up on getting
some kind of signal from me, and I get a voice, a human
live voice, and it says: 'How may I help you?' Just like the
old times! I give them my name and I read out my long
number to them, and ask for my balance—but they don't
trust my voice. They ask for my Social Security number.
I have it written on the front of my checkbook too. Then
they ask for the amount of my last deposit. That takes some
scrambling, but I finally find it, and then they give me my
balance, just as nice as you please. And do you know something? They're right, every time!"

September 10th

Lucille has arranged for our little pen pals to come out
to us this Saturday for a picnic at the duck pond. Amanda
wrote me:

> Dear Mrs. McNair,
>   I will be so glad to meet you on Saterday.
> That will be neat. I will grin and you will
> know me because my tooth is not back in yet.
>   Yesterday a boy in my class fell down at
> recess and broke his arm. Maybe its not relly
> broke, just bent a little. I hope so.
>   Love,
>   Amanda

I detect a good heart in this child. I, too, am looking forward to Saturday.

September 11th

Curtis and Paul just provided me with a delightful half hour of after-dinner conversation—they on one side of the library window and I on the other!

The "prize-winner" story tonight was about a couple whom Curtis called George and Mary. Seems they were sitting on their front porch and saw a man and a woman come out of the house across the street. As they watched, the man turned and gave the woman a resounding kiss.

"Oh, George," said Mary wistfully to her husband, "why don't you do that?"

"Why, honey," replied George, "I don't even *know* that lady!"

Strictly speaking, Dear Diary, I know I'm eavesdropping, but I feel a bit like I'm sitting with Sam at the end of the day as I did so many pleasant evenings of our marriage. He had a rare sense of humor. A little earthy, but not too much so.... I treasure those memories—and am thankful for the present company of these two entertaining gentlemen. Not all treasures in this place are made of paper and hidden away. *Deo gratias.*

4

Win Some, Lose Some

September 14th

The picnic was a big success. The six children (all girls; Mrs. Trotter couldn't persuade a single boy to be a "correspondent") were shy at first, but after we taught them the game of Blind Man's Bluff we were all laughing. I was astonished to learn that these children had never played that!

Amanda was even more adorable than I had thought she would be, with short curly brown hair, bright hazel eyes, and dimples. We ate our lunch side by side on a small bench overlooking the pond. After hearing Lucille address me as "Miss Hattie," Amanda was soon calling me that, and chatting away.

Voices mean so much. Hers was soft, not the least bit strident as she told me about her dog and her cat and the spelling bee they had just had at school.

"I missed out on 'hospital.' I put too many *s*'s in it," she said. "I made it 'hoss-pistol'!" She giggled and put her hand over her mouth. I said I thought "hospital" was a right hard word for the third grade. She squeezed my hand and gave me a grateful smile. A truly fetching child. I hope she enjoyed the outing half as much as I did.

September 15th

There is a new bone of contention in our establishment.

Years ago an artist (the son of a resident here, I think) gave The Home a large, original painting of water lilies in a Lowcountry pond, complete with cypress trees and two egrets hovering over the quiet scene. It has hung above the mantel in the dining room as long as I can remember. When the gas logs were lit in winter, the painted scene was highlighted. It was serene and beautiful. We loved it.

Suddenly this morning, the picture was gone! That was not the worst part. In its place was an oil portrait of a man—a gentleman, I suppose—at least he was well dressed and his black hair was severely combed; but the word "gentleman" to me denotes a gentle man, and this he did not look to be. He looked hard-faced, as if he did not care for what he was seeing.... One thing was sure: we didn't care for what *we* were seeing.

Our administrator was eating lunch at a corner table. We converged on him, demanding an explanation.

"Folks," he said, trying to be pleasant, "I knew you'd raise a ruckus, and I can't say as I blame you; but you've just got to accept the situation. That—er—gentleman is Asa Purifoy, the grandfather of Nelson Purifoy, who as you probably know is the president of the Purifoy Corporation. They own and operate this home, as well as a number of others. 'Mr. Nelson,' as we call him, is a real nice man, with a lot of family feeling; and he has decided that a copy of his grandfather's portrait should hang in a prominent place at each of the homes, since he started the company in 1948. There you have it." Mr. Detwiler took a deep breath and shrugged his shoulders.

We just looked at him helplessly.

"They tell me he was a smart man." Mr. D. was still struggling.

"Smart and mean?" commented Cecil.

"No. I think he just had a poor portrait painter."

"You're just being generous.... Where is our water lily painting?"

"It was hung in a good place, on the wall of E Hall," said Mr. Detwiler.

"We have to give up that nice painting," Cecil protested, shaking his head, "and look instead at this old guy who looks so mean he takes away our appetites. He looks like something he ate didn't agree with him.... I think I'll call Mr. Purifoy 'Ole Pukey Face.'"

Some of the ladies shook their heads at that moniker. They don't like the P-word. I'm not crazy about it myself, but I have a feeling the name will stick.

September 17th

Cecil's name for the portrait got around quickly. I heard several derogatory comments today about "Ole Pukey Face." He looks down on us malevolently. We make faces back at him and long for our beloved water lilies; but of course there's nothing we can do about it. R.H.I.P.—"Rank Has Its Privileges."

September 19th

There are some people here who fix light breakfasts and suppers in their kitchenettes and only go into the dining room for their midday meal. With many of them this is their only social contact in twenty-four hours, and they are inclined to draw it out, stretching the dessert and coffee as far as they can. Sometimes you can sense that people are reaching for subjects to extend the conversation.

Today, for instance, Sue said, "Marcia, I was taking a walk yesterday afternoon and I saw that vine you have on your trellis." (Marcia lives in one of The Home's cottages.) "It's already blazing with fall color."

"Isn't it, though? I love that vine," said Marcia, "especially in autumn. I planted it and nursed it along—and now I can't even remember the name of it!"

Louly spoke up. "Isn't there a vine called Kentucky Wonder?"

"No," said Marcia. "That's not it.... But I think it has the name of a state in it.... A Southern state—"

"Virginia Creeper!" shouted Sue.

"He looks like something he ate didn't agree with
him. I think I'll call him 'Ole Pukey Face.'"

We actually clapped. We were so pleased to arrive at the name of one state's vine, even if it was by way of another state's string bean. A nice little victory. We don't have many mental victories these days.

Later

In my mail today came a prompt note of thanks from Amanda for the picnic:

> Dear Miss Hattie,
> I was glad to meet you at the picnic. You are a real neat lady. I am glad Mrs. Trotter picked me out to be your pen pal.
> Love,
> Amanda
> PS My friend Lily is home sick. I think she has amonia, but not a very bad case.

September 23rd

The McLeans are the most devoted couple at The Home. It does me good to see them, to know they have been married for fifty-two years and still find each other's company not only bearable but superior to that of anyone else!

The last lines from an old song always come to my mind when I see the way Gracie looks at Wallace:

> ...No, the heart that has truly loved never forgets,
> But as truly loves on to the close;
> As the sunflower turns to her god, when he sets,
> The same look that she turned when he rose.

Those were Thomas Moore's sentiments, expressed a century and a half ago, in a song that begins, "Believe me, if all those endearing young charms...." He must have loved happy-faced sunflowers as much as I do. He also wrote movingly about another flower: "The last rose of summer, left blooming all alone."

How I would have liked to have known that gentleman, with his soft, sentimental heart and his facile pen!

That started me to thinking about other people I wish I could have met, if only long enough to try to thank them for all the joy they have brought to my eyes and ears and mind, as well as to my heart and soul: Michelangelo and Tchaikovsky and Massenet and Chopin and Robert Burns and Dickens and James Hilton and Charles Kuralt, and dozens of others. I feel an almost crushing indebtedness. There should be *some* way to make *some* kind of payment....

September 25th

A new resident was moving into an apartment in my wing on the second floor yesterday. I wasn't being nosy; I happened to walk down the hall just as the movers were leaving, taking with them the headboard, footboard, and mattress of a mahogany bed. The new tenant stood in her doorway, watching them and weeping.

"Can I help you?" I asked.

She wiped her eyes and shook her head. I started to move on, but she touched my arm and motioned me to come inside. She got hold of herself and offered me a chair in her cluttered living room.

"You see," she said, in a shaky voice, "they found that my double bed wouldn't fit in the bedroom. They say I will have to get a single one." She blew her nose and looked out at the treetops.

I introduced myself and told her we were glad she had come to live with us.

"I'm Amy Blackburn," she said. "I'm glad too, I *think*.... Right now I'm sick at heart. I can sleep on my sofa bed tonight, but...that bed! It was Dick's and mine since we were married, fifty-four years ago. He's gone now...and I can't *bear*...to part...with *our bed*."

She started to cry again. I hugged her and slipped out, murmuring something about coming back later. I decided she needed a little grieving time, alone.

Grieving time. There's so *much* of it, when life begins to wind down. Not only grieving for faces we will never look on again, but for *things*—things we have loved and lost, or have had to leave behind—the dear, familiar furnishings of our existence.

I was more fortunate than Amy, with my bed. The rooms of my apartment are larger than hers, and I was able to keep the walnut double bed that has been my resting place for nearly six decades, since Sam and I bought it in a secondhand shop for ten dollars. We had a carpenter split the side boards and lengthen them by six inches, so there was room to stretch. It showed its antique strength later on when four children would pile in on us every Sunday morning, for a family frolic and love fest. I was always afraid the slats would give way, but they didn't.... Oh, dear. Poor Amy Blackburn.

Later

Brooding on our new resident and the sacrifice of her beloved bed made me think of something that has always made me cry: the scenes in westward-ho movies when women on the wagon trains were told that the wagons' loads must be lightened, that anything not a dire necessity must be "pitched." It broke my heart to see those brave, tired, and discouraged women part with a dainty little table or a rocking chair, or a pan of dirt planted with cuttings of rose bushes and vines—precious belongings and reminders of home, all tossed out to the dismal prairie and cried over as the wagons lurched away.

Oh, my. There is much talk these days about making everything equal for everybody. I wonder if anything will ever be done about the heartaches that women bear in this world—a very unequal share, it seems to me.

Overheard: "I have good days and bad days, and sometimes I can't tell the difference."

That reminds me of something that George Bernard Shaw quoted: "In troubled times Oscar Wilde maintained his 'gaiety of soul.'"

If I have any "gaiety of soul" left, I must try to maintain it.

September 29th

Phoebe Long, our newest cottage resident, was born and raised in Massachusetts. Like so many Navy people, she and her husband settled in Drayton after his last tour of duty at the Charleston Naval Base. He died last year. I like her immensely, even though she is different from most of us in this place, in several ways. She is neater, more orderly in her life and thinking, or so it seems to me. And I don't believe she is as church-oriented or as religious as many Southern women are; but I could be wrong.

Phoebe and I came out of the chapel together this morning after attending a memorial service for poor old Theodora, who passed away peacefully on Friday. Theo had been so terribly mixed up and so utterly miserable lately that we could only be glad about her release.

Walking along under the pine trees, Phoebe and I began to talk about death.

"Does the thought of it scare you?" I asked.

"Not really," she said; and then she told me about hearing Katharine Hepburn being interviewed on television, several years ago. The interviewer asked her if she feared death.

"Not in the least," said Miss Hepburn, serenely. "If there is life after death, that's fine. If not, I will be asleep—and I love to sleep."

"That's now my philosophy," said Phoebe, smiling. She seems quite content with it.

Later

I've been thinking about Phoebe and her philosophy. I'm not much of an evangelist, but I feel I must try to find a way to let her know what a comfort it is to be *sure* of a life after death.

September 30th

Eloise gave us a good laugh at the table today. Somehow the talk had turned to a rather strange phenomenon we'd been hearing about lately: so many women in their forties giving birth.

Eloise said, "Humph! Their forties? That's nothing. I was fifty when my Jimmy was born. Best mistake I ever made!"

Then Cecil told a naughty one. He said a man, eighty-one years old, paid a visit to his doctor. A few days later the doctor, driving through the park, spied his patient in bright orange shorts, jogging with a flamboyant young female with bright red hair. The doctor stopped them, looked at the man, and said, "What do you think you're doing?"

"Well, Doc, you told me to get a hot mama!"

"I didn't say, 'Get a hot mama.' I said, 'You've got a heart murmur!'"

Since I've put down that immodest story tonight, I'll put down another one. They tell me that this happened at another home. At a midweek vespers service a visiting minister talked about religious music, about hymns, old and new. He said, "Hymns are so varied. There's a hymn about nearly everything. To prove it, I want someone to call out a word and see if somebody else can come up with a hymn related to that subject."

After a minute a man called out, "Wood." Quickly someone replied, "The Old Rugged Cross."

Someone else said, "Water." Immediately a woman answered with "Shall We Gather at the River?"

Somebody boldly said, "Sex." There was quiet for a minute. Then a little gray-haired lady looked timidly at the aged husband sitting beside her and offered in a low voice, "Precious Memories, How They Linger." Whooo-eeee.

October 1st

I saw Arthur—and Dolly—coming out of Mr. Detwiler's office this morning, and they looked upset. Of course, I had to inquire.

It seems that a neighbor who lives behind Kudzu Kottage (one, it turns out, who has complained about the children playing on "his property") now says that the garden spot lies partly on his land. The Priests started "bush-hogging" (I must find out later what in the world that is!) the area last weekend, and the man threatened to call the sheriff.

They decided to talk to Mr. D., who is just as outraged as I am. He is going to talk to The Home's attorney and try to get the matter straightened out. Surely justice will prevail, and that crotchety antagonist will reap what mean-spiritedness he is sowing.

Later

I could not find "bush-hogging" in any dictionary, not even the unabridged one in the library. So when the telephone rates went down, I called my gardener son to inquire (and to chat). He informed me that it is a term for heavy-duty mowing, the kind of mowing that must be done when underbrush is overgrown.

It is so true that you can learn something new every day.

5

Sights to See

October 2nd

What a to-do! When we were taking our places at breakfast this morning somebody pointed to the wall above the fireplace.

"Look! He's gone! Ole Pukey Face is gone!"

Sure enough, the wall was as bare as the day it was painted! We looked at each other, and somebody started clapping. Soon we were a clapping, rejoicing family. Oh, boy! The bugaboo had disappeared.

We wondered. Had Mr. Nelson Purifoy relented?

We soon learned from Mr. Detwiler that such was not the case. "The portrait was stolen last night," he said.

"Stolen?" we asked. "Who would want it?"

He shrugged his shoulders. He looked worried. "We are

instituting a thorough search. I hope each of you will co-operate with us in this matter," he said, frowning. "If the painting is not located soon, I will have to notify the Charlotte office." Poor man.

We were sorry for him, but delighted for ourselves. That bare wall looked great. We had high hopes that the water lilies would eventually be restored to us.

I guess Mr. Asa Purifoy's portrait is not the only less-than-pleasing sight we are subjected to. I passed through the lobby about two o'clock this afternoon and saw Eloise sprawled in one of the lounge chairs near the TV, her knees apart, flabby thighs exposed. Her head was thrown back with her mouth wide open, a lovely sight for anyone coming into our establishment from the outside world. She even snores.

I understand the management has spoken to her, but they got nowhere. "The very idea!" she said indignantly. "I'm not sleeping in the lobby! I'm looking at my soap opera. If my eyes close occasionally, what harm is that?"

Our main meal is midday, and Eloise eats heartily. I have found that old people—myself included—are like babies: fill our stomachs and we "drop off." The trouble is, we often drop off when we don't want to. Sam and I used to pick out plays or good old movies to watch in the evening on television. Many, many times when they would play the "ending music" loudly, I would wake up and say, "Oh, Sam! Do tell me what happened? How did it end?" He'd shake himself awake and say, "How do *I* know?"

Later—another "sight to see"

Edward T., a nice man, is rail thin. Most people gain weight when they move here, but he has lost some. He keeps on losing. His pants are getting looser and looser. Somebody nicknamed him "Droopy-Drawers," but no one calls him that to his face. He manages to stay dignified, even though his belt is not tight enough.

Tonight I saw him coming into the dining room, and it looked as if his pants were going to slip down any minute over his skinny hips and thighs.

Somebody said, "Uh-oh. We're gonna get mooned."

"What's 'mooned'?" Susan asked.

Cecil said, "You'll find out if he bends over."

October 3rd

Retta came for a cup of tea this afternoon, and we talked about the notes I kept to let her know what life at FairAcres was like—when she was trying to decide if it was time for her to move out of her house. Those "jottings" turned into my first little book, and now my wee second novel is "going to town." The publisher tells me that there will have to be another printing soon.

And the letters keep coming, more than three hundred now! Retta and I perused some of them and marveled at my unlikely new "career."

I was nervous about book number two. What if the first one—now in its sixth printing—had just been a fluke? Suppose it contained all that people wanted to hear about life in a Southern retirement home, and the second one fell flat?

Well, it hasn't happened. Many of the lovely people who wrote me nicely about the first book are now writing me nicely about the second. I answered every one of those first letters. Now, Dear Diary, do you think I should write to those same people again? Some of them have been kind enough to say, "Don't feel that you have to answer this. Just write us another book." So, dear ones, I'm trying.

I will ask my readers, as I've asked them before, not to look for an involved plot. Not many consequential things happen in our sheltered lives. However, once in a while there's a little twist of fate, a little bump in the path, as we trudge along. I will keep my pencil at the ready.

October 6th

Another cute letter came from Amanda today.

> Dear Miss Hattie,
>
> Today is Saterday and I am spose to clean my room. That is not any fun. If I close my eyes I cant see the mess any more but I cant go around with my eyes shut all day. So, I decided to write to you insted.
>
> I did better on the spelling bee yesterday. I was hoping the teacher would give me hospital again. See, I can spell it now.
>
> My friend Susie made an F in Conduct. If I ever came home with F in Conduct there woudnt be anything left of me but crums. (Just kidding.)
>
> Love,
> Amanda

October 10th

Mr. Detwiler has had a success. (Not in finding the portrait, though I'm sure he would have to consider finding it a success.) The matter of the garden spot has been resolved. It seems that Arthur's complaining neighbor has a history of cantankerousness and has absolutely no claim on the property in question. The sheriff has, indeed, paid a visit— though not the one threatened—and doesn't think there will be any more problems. He considers the old man a harmless fellow.

Arthur plans to clear and plow the ground before the really cold weather so some planting can be done early next spring. A "posse" of residents, with visions of vine-ripened tomatoes in their heads, have offered to "guard" the operation if needed, but let's hope it doesn't come to that!

October 11th

A visitor came up to me yesterday in the lobby, all "bright-eyed and bushy-tailed," and said those ugly words: "I'll bet you don't know who I am!"

Oooh, how I hate that approach. It's unkind and uncouth. I'm no good at remembering names, *any*time, and especially in a sudden confrontation.

Last night I lay in bed and figured out the quip I'm going to have ready—next time.

Confronter: "I'll bet you don't know who I am!"

Me (with a big, if insincere, smile): "No, but I'm just as glad to see you as if I did!"

George Burns and Gracie Allen were so good with quips and comebacks. A quote I ran across recently showed me that George also knew one of the secrets to growing old gracefully: "I feel sorry for people who live in the past. I know it was cheaper then, and I know that some people had very interesting pasts, but you can't keep looking in a rearview mirror—unless you enjoy having a stiff neck. Old memories are fine, but you have still got time to make new memories."

Later

There's something that worries me, or rather confuses me: the way certain collective nouns that are treated as singular in America are treated as plural in England. For instance, "The Government have decided..." or "The Ministry wish us to...."

The other day in an English novel I read the following exchange:

"Whom do I root for?"

"Well, England are playing Australia, but one does not root."

England are. That bowled me over. I'm going to have to write to a grammar expert and find out which country is (are?) correct.

October 13th

I had another letter from Amanda today.

Dear Miss Hattie,
   I hope you are doing fine. I am doing fine.
A lady came to school today to talk to us in Main
Hall about Oldin Times. She was nice but kind of
rinkle-dy. Melvin sat behind me and I herd him
say she is so old her skin don't fit right any more.
I hope she didn't hear him.
   I bet you could tell us more about Oldin Times
than she could.
   Please write me soon.
                                        Love,
                                        Amanda

   Children have a way of putting us in our places. As
Amanda indicates, about all I can talk about any more is
(are??) "oldin times"; and every time I look in the mirror
now I touch my skin and remember Melvin's remark.

October 19th

   I came up with a new rhyme last night. It was born of a
frustration that, I think, many have experienced.

   SPACE AGE BOTTLE
   They make me feel so immature—
   Incapable of learning—
   Those child-resistant bottle tops
   That say, "Press down while turning."
   You have to have three hands, or else
   A grandchild you can call.
   He twists his little wrist, and look!
   It's off! No sweat a-tall!

October 21st

When I went to our library today to return a book, I found Paul sitting there at the large table with pen, notebook, and thesaurus.

"I'm working on my list of car names," he said.

"Well, you really *are* serious about the contest," I replied.

"Hattie, I'll tell you. I've gotten real caught up in this thing. It's a good time-passer."

"Right. And it helps to get the rust off the wheels. Last night I thought of a couple of names to give you. I wrote them down or they'd have been long gone." I pulled out my trusty little notebook and read: "Eagle, Courser, Gazelle."

"They'd be fine, Hattie, if this were a sports car. Before I saw a picture of the car I had thought of Nimble, Clout, Rigadoon, Jamboree, Tantivy.... I like Tantivy, don't you?"

"*Love* it. Goodness, I don't think I've heard that word for 'galloping' since my father died."

"But those names don't suit this machine." He showed me the contest's entry blank, which he had sent off for. Pictured was a sedan, elegant and refined-looking. "It's an upper-crust family car. Somehow that makes it harder to name. This morning I've only come up with Rhapsody, Melody, Elation, and Halcyon."

"Ooh, I like Halcyon. Do send that in. How many names can you submit?"

"Three.... There's something else to think of, Hattie. I've been out of things in the advertising world for several years; plus, I haven't kept up with new car models. There may already be a Halcyon, or a Rhapsody, running around."

"Maybe, but I don't think so.... Only three names. That really narrows it down. I'd have a terrible time deciding which three. But you'll do it, Paul. Good luck, old dear."

I found the book I was looking for and left the library feeling uplifted. It's good when one of our number stirs up his gray matter and attempts to accomplish something more than just staying alive.

Later

Overheard, Cecil to Sidney:

"Last week I paid $2,700 for two new hearing aids. I told that fella I'd better hear some larruppin' good stuff, or I'd sue him."

"Have you heard any?"

"Nah. Just the same old junk, a little louder."

October 23rd

Nearly every night at supper, they give us some kind of fruit to take home. Last night it was apples. Lucius turned his shiny Red Delicious around and around in his hands. With a sigh, he said, "When I was a young boy I thought apples were the most beautiful things in the world. Then, a few years later, I discovered girls, and I thought they were the most beautiful things in the world.... Now I'm eighty-four, and I'm back to apples." Lucius shook his head mournfully. When we laughed, he decided to amuse us further.

"Hey, I heard about a fella who began to have trouble remembering names. Know anybody like that? Anyway, he met a friend with the same trouble, on the street.

"'Hello, friend,' he said. 'I read in the obituary column this morning that either you or your brother died.'

"'Oh?' said the friend. 'Which one was it?'"

We laughed again, which may have been a mistake, because he went on.

"I heard about a man who went to his doctor and said he was having trouble with his sex life. The doctor, a great believer in exercise, said, 'Walk ten miles a day for seven days, and then call me.'

"He followed the doctor's orders and when he called, the doctor said, 'How is your sex life?'

"'How can I know?' answered the man. 'I'm seventy miles from home!'"

October 24th

Taking advantage of a gloriously sunny autumn day, Paul and Curtis were already talking and smoking away when I slipped into my place in the library after lunch to eavesdrop.

"Well, I've been thinking about it, Paul," I heard Curtis say, "and I believe your best bet would be to name that car 'Stallion.' That's a strong name, and maybe it would interest the ladies!"

Paul whooped. "I wish I had the nerve!" he said.

It's plain that those two enjoy each other's company. Sometimes they sit for a long while saying nothing, probably just enjoying the quiet in this peaceful spot. During those times I get some reading done. When they speak again my ears perk up.

"Hey, Paul," said Curtis, after a bit, "do you know how you can tell you're at a South Carolina Lowcountry wedding?"

"No. How?"

"When they throw red rice."

I chuckled, thinking of our wonderful Rice Pilau, with tomatoes in it.

Paul said, "I can take that further. When they go to a wedding where it's plain that the couple is already expecting, they throw puffed rice!"

"Tsk, tsk," said Curtis. "What are we coming to?"

October 30th

Amanda has frequently mentioned a boy named Melvin in her letters. I begin to feel that I know him. She once reported,

> Melvin brought Teacher a butiful apple yesterday. He kept looking at it on her desk. On his way out to lunch he took the apple back and ate it. How about that? Melvin is a mess.
>
> One day while Mrs. Trotter was out of the room he stud on a table and took a yard stick and terned the hands of the clock ahead. He thought we would get out sooner, but we didnt.

In another letter she said,

> We have a lot of caterpillows in our school yard. Yesterday I tried to make a pet out of one at recess. I named him Clarence and

cleared a place for him to craul but Melvin
came by and stepped on him and smushed
him. That was mean. Boys can be so mean.

Amanda is taking me back to my school days. I remember my third-grade class, and a boy who sat behind me and put things down the back of my dress....

November 1st

At first there was much talk about the disappearance of the portrait, or as somebody called the caper: The Purloining of Ole Pukey Face. It had taken place—nearly a month ago now—between the time the kitchen closed, about eight in the evening, and the time it opened, before breakfast, around six. All the workers were interrogated thoroughly. No one had seen or heard anything out of the ordinary.

Our night watchman was, of course, the first person called on the carpet. He, Mr. Carpenter, a reliable and well-liked man, a retired school teacher, declared that he had made his rounds on his bicycle, as usual, and had noticed nothing amiss anywhere on the campus. It was a dark, rainy night, which may have made it easier for the culprits to carry out their mission.

Poor Mr. Detwiler. He eventually had to report the matter to the headquarters office. Mr. Nelson Purifoy came down, grim-faced, and took part in the search and interrogation.

To our great glee, no portrait has been found.

November 3rd

I cannot help but think that *someone* knows the story of the stolen portrait—or someones, plural. But there has not been a smidgen of gossip as far as my fairly sharp ears have heard. Anyone involved knows how to keep quiet.

Cora told us today about a woman in her hometown named Katy who was always getting into trouble by talking too much.

One Sunday night at vespers service, during sentence prayers, Cora heard Katy say aloud, "Please, Lord, I beg you, put your arms around my shoulders and your hand over my mouth."

Good for Katy. There are many of us who should duplicate her prayer.

6

—

Cloudy and Bright

November 7th

The clothes in my closet are complaining. They're being cruelly squashed.

I've been saying it for two years: I've *got* to get rid of some dresses and suits before their wrinkles turn into *rigor mortis.*

This morning I took out a few things and threw them on the bed. I could almost hear them sighing with relief at being un-squashed for even a minute. I put a box on the floor to fill with offerings for Goodwill.

The first thing I began to put in the box was a grape-colored knit suit. Grape is not my best color. Purple makes my cheeks look hag-ish. Still, I recalled as I looked at it, the suit fits me nicely. The long top hides the dewlaps around my middle. I remembered wearing it once last winter....

I decided I had to think about it, and I started a "Think-About" pile.

Then I pulled out the pink chiffon that I wore to my grandson's evening wedding, nine years ago. I had kept it, hoping for another such occasion, but none of my other "grands" show any signs of nuptializing—which is sad for me, great-grandchildren-wise. I laid the pretty, soft, flattering dress in the Goodwill box with a sigh. I hope another grandmother will come upon it at the Goodwill outlet, buy it, and wear it to a happy wedding.

I haven't worn slacks in years, even though on some cold days I could relish their warmth. They do nothing to enhance my figure (what's left of it). And yet I found four pairs still taking up space in this clothes warren, two of them woolen. I believe, in the back of my mind, there was the thought that if we ever had ice and snow again, as we had in The Great Ice Storm of 1962 (a memorable phenomenon in South Carolina) I would need something over my legs. Oh, dear. I've waited well over thirty years for another phenomenon. That's long enough. I dropped all four pairs into the box.

I don't know whether or not El Niño has caused it, but we haven't had any really cold winter weather here for seven or eight years, and yet—there hung three winter coats. Not to mention a spring coat and a raincoat. I was definitely over-coated. After soul-searching deliberation I put two of the heavy coats into the box.

I still have some misgivings about parting with that blue mohair job, now folded into the Goodwill box. It's a handsome coat, and I've had it for twelve years. Have worn it about four times during those years—but at least I knew it was *there*. Oh, me.

By then it was time to go to lunch. I jammed the rest of the clothes back into the closet, with the Think-About items at one end. There's still not room for the garments to shake out their wrinkles properly, but maybe they can breathe a little better. Maybe I can, too.

I marched off to lunch with a clearer conscience.

November 10th

Thanksgiving is coming, and some of us were talking about how much we have to be thankful for.

"Well," said Elsie, after a while, "I've got a lot *not* to be thankful for, like my wobbly knee and two cataracts, and paths of pink scalp showing through my thin hair—those, on top of emphysema and macular degeneration and osteoporosis. But there's one good thing: I don't have any dandruff!"

So then, for a while, we had to do a little "venting" about some of our ailments.

One of the mean things that a scheming Mother Nature has thought up to do to us poor old "seniors" is to shrink us. No matter how straight I try to stand, I'm about two inches shorter than I used to be. Even my arms have shrunk! Now how could *that* have happened? My sleeves hang halfway over my hands. Awkward and messy.

Even worse is the cloudiness over everything. Cora is to have a cataract removed next week. She has high hopes of seeing clearly again, but it doesn't always work out that way.

Two friends of mine have discovered macular degeneration after cataract removals. Cora is ready to try anything, though. "I can't stand the cloudiness any longer," she said. "I'm tired of this murkiness—of living in the shadows."

I know what she means. There are so many clouds at our age. Our eyes are cloudy from cataracts; our ears are cloudy from something—maybe hearing too much; our minds are cloudy from—what? Overuse, or being overfilled with junk?

Anyway, all of this sometimes makes for an overcast existence: murky, dingy, shady. And after writing all this down I find myself gloomy, and badly in need of a pick-me-up.... I wonder whatever happened to Hadacol?

Many things get harder and harder to accomplish as the years roll on, such as filing the nails on my right hand, pulling up a long zipper on the back of a dress, bending my bad knee enough to step into my panties, trying to read the ridiculously small numbers in the telephone book....

And even little irksome things seem harder to bear, like waiting for the red light to change, waiting in lines at checkout counters, waiting for a boring person to come to the end of a long, boring account....

The poet John Dryden told us to "possess our souls with patience." As my soul ages, patience seems harder and harder to possess.

Later

Tonight I was trying to go through all my knee exercises. I'm afraid I have gotten lax about doing them every day. There is still talk from time to time about a swimming pool.

It would be beneficial to many of us.

"When night draws on I want my night drawers on." Now where in the world did I hear *that?*

November 12th

A delegation from the Residents' Council approached Mr. Detwiler today and asked that our beautiful Lowcountry painting be restored to its old place in the dining room.

At first he hesitated; then he said, "I made it known to Mr. Purifoy that you-all had grown attached to the water-color that had been there for many years, and that you were missing it. Maybe he won't object to your having it back.... I'm not sure...but...go ahead. Move it back. We'll see what happens." Dear Mr. D. He has to put up with so much, from so many quarters.

We thanked him profusely and arranged for Arthur and a helper to return our water lilies to their rightful place. They seem more beautiful than ever.

It was while a number of us were looking up at our re-claimed painting today, and rejoicing over it, that I happened to catch a look that passed between two of our male residents—something that I wasn't supposed to see, but did. A smug look. Maybe even a wink.

As if I had been hit on the head, I knew, right that minute, that those two men—who have always been slightly on the devilish side—knew more about the theft than they had told anybody. I sidled over to where they were, dying for them to "clue me in"—but I couldn't get up the nerve to come right out and ask them.... Maybe they will decide to tell me, when more time has passed.... Meantime, the mystery remains completely and utterly unsolved.

November 16th

A female resident came into church service in the chapel this morning looking extremely lumpy around the shoulders. Apparently there were very large shoulder pads inside her dress and inside her jacket, and they added up to unnatural mounds.

It made me think of my Sam. He hated for women to wear big shoulder pads. Whenever he thought I was over-upholstered in the shoulder area he would say, "Are you tryin' to look like a Clemson fullback?"

I remember taking out some pads, and being pleased that he even noticed.

November 17th

I sat in the library this afternoon near the window, hoping Paul and Curtis would come to their usual chairs on the terrace and take advantage of the warmest part of the day, and they did.

After a few quiet minutes of relaxing, Curtis said, "I heard something kinda funny on Friday. I had to go to Charleston to the doctor. Herbie drove me down, and we parked near a construction site. You know, they're always puttin' up something new at that medical complex. Anyway, I heard a foreman—bound to be a Lowcountry fella—yell in the direction of two young guys leanin' against a fence.

"'Come here, you, boy!' he said.

"'Which one of us you callin'?' one of the fellas asked.

"'Don't matter,' the foreman answered. 'All two of you jest as worse.'"

Paul chuckled. He enjoys Curtis's stories, as do I.

After a quiet interval, Curtis said, "Any new ideas for that car-namin' contest?"

"You bet. It's fun. Gets some of the rust off my creaky brain cells. Wanta hear some names I thought of today?"

"Sure.... Wait, let me adjust this darn hearing aid."

I could hear Paul rattling a piece of paper. "OK. Here are the latest possibilities: Premier, Trophy, Elegy, Caprice, Yeoman, Symphony."

"They sound pretty good.... I still think somethin' with a little zing—a little muscle—would be better...like...well, like Shorthorn or Mastiff...or how about Vixen? Matter of fact, I still like Stallion."

I left them laughing over that.

November 18th

Sometimes after a day filled more than normally with aches and pains and tiredness and memories that make me sad, I hear a still, small voice in the back of my mind saying, "You've lived too long, old girl. You've passed the point of usefulness and enjoyment. You're just taking up space— an aching space, most of the time. That's your trouble."

And I suppose it is. Antibiotics have killed *pneumococci* and other germs that would have carried me off in days not so "olden." I remember when my dear friend Sarah Moorer died, how pneumonia shortened and lessened her suffering, saving her from a lingering death from throat cancer. She had written instructions about her wishes for health care; I have followed her example.

So there are mixed feelings. But when "the hill" looms, there's one thing I can do that is sure to cheer. I can pull down from a shelf two large boxes that contain more than three hundred letters that have come to me, totally unexpected letters that have stunned me with their kind words about my two little books.

When I read, "Do make us laugh again," and "I can hardly wait for Number Three," I take a deep breath, drink a can of Ensure, and follow it up with some coffee. Then I pick up my pen and notebook and ramble through that part of my brain where the *good* memories go. Soon I'm remembering and jotting, grinning over something I once heard. Like this story about an Army recruit filling out a questionnaire on health:

Question: "What are rabies, and what can be done about them?"

Recruit's answer: "Rabies are Jewish priests, and you can't do nothing about them."

As to that hill, I will try to go over it laughing.

Later

Here are some words of wit I have overheard lately at this Residence of Relics:

"The Mason-Dixon Line? Sure, I know what it is. It's the line that divides 'Y'all' from 'Youse guys.'"

"I remember a sign the general posted on the bulletin board at the Army camp I had the pleasure of attending in 1942: There will be no more unauthorized stealing at this camp!"

"Guess what? Mary and I finally finished putting together that jigsaw puzzle last night—the flower-garden one."

"How long did it take you?"

"Let's see...'bout four months. That's not too bad, either. The front of the box says two to four years."

Still later

Our doctor comes to The Home twice a week for appointments. Meantime, the nurses in the clinic and the infirmary call him when necessary. Fortunately, for him and for us, he has a sense of humor. Recently a nurse called and told him that one of our ladies, in taking a walk on the campus, had played with a rabbit, and the rabbit bit her.

The doctor said, "Put some antibiotic ointment on the wound. That ought to do it. Oh—and call me if she starts to hop!"

November 19th

Some of us put out the word that there would be a meeting Wednesday morning (today) in the library to talk about ways and means of making money to help build a swimming pool.

We've given up on expecting Management to build it, and we're now working on the faint hope that if we raise part of the money, they might feel compelled to come up with the rest.

Paul and Curtis both came, and Sidney and Retta were there. I invited Amy Blackburn, especially. She and I have discovered several interests in common since the tearful meeting over her too-large bed.

The group talked about things like fashion shows, silver teas, croquet contests, but there wasn't much enthusiasm.

"The best things we've had here in years," said Sidney, "were the two Recollection Nights, the Memory Nights."

Everyone nodded. "You're exactly right," said Marcia. "But do we want to do that *again?* Isn't twice enough?"

"Not for me!" shouted Curtis. "I could listen to you-all's memories from now till Christmas."

"Here's an idea," said Cora. "Maybe we could write down our funny or touching recollections, and somebody could type them up and copy them and bind them somehow."

"That's a good thought, Cora," said Retta.

"But," pointed out Sidney, "it would mean an awful lot of work, *if* we could get people to do it. Some people who can roll a rich tale out of their mouths simply aren't any good at writing it down. They're daunted by pen and paper.... Maybe we could charge five or six dollars for the bound copies that you're talking about.... But somehow I don't think it would be as much fun or as lucrative as the Memory Nights. A number of people got so carried away with the tales told on those evenings that they dropped twenty-five dollars—or more—in the pot!"

"Right," said Curtis. "I'd give that much to hear Paul tell the story again about Horace the Mule. There's just something about hearin' it...instead of readin' it."

"It just seems too bad that we can't come up with something a little different," said Cora.

"Does anybody have any ideas about how we could vary the 'Evening'?" asked Paul.

"Well, we could give it a different name," Curtis suggested. "We could say that it's not just memories, but handed-down stories too." He thought for a minute; then his face lit up. "How about 'Tales and Taradiddles'?"

"I like that," said Paul.

"What's a taradiddle?" somebody inquired.

"It's a story that 'ain't necessarily so,'" said Curtis. "That would give us a lot of leeway."

"Here's an idea," suggested Retta. "How about inviting family and friends…and maybe people from town? I'll bet they'd love it!"

"Good thinking, Retta!" said Paul.

It was agreed that we would start our fund-raising campaign with the "Tales" night, and follow it up with some of the other ideas we had discussed, and perhaps plan a rummage sale and a costume party. The storytelling is to take place in early spring. That should give us time to dig up many a true tale from our pasts, or our parents' pasts, and happily a few outrageous taradiddles.

Just before we finished, Amy Blackburn spoke up. "I'm so new here, maybe I shouldn't make a suggestion. But it occurs to me that there must be many good recipes known to this crowd—good family-food concoctions passed down from grandmothers. If they could be gathered together into a cookbook with a catchy name—"

"That's a great idea, Amy!" I said, and meant it. There was a nodding of heads.

Sidney said, "We'll surely work on that one, Amy—right after the storytelling night. Let's work on that first. Everybody get busy now. Dig into your memories. Deep."

November 20th

This letter came from Amanda today.

Dear Miss Hattie,
    We had Show and Tell at school today, and gess who I talked about??? YOU! I showed them the picture of you and me taken at the picnic with the ducks eating the crums. I told them that you have written two books and they want to meet you. Will you come to our school some day? That would be neat.
                        Love,
                        Amanda

Well, I suppose I will have to go. I want to please that dear child—but what will I talk about to third-graders? I haven't been one in about seventy years. That's a *long* time. I'll call Mrs. Trotter, their teacher, to see if she knows about this idea.

Oh—and I'll talk to Louly. She was a teacher...one of those people truly called to that profession, I must say. What a wonderful thing she did a couple of years ago in teaching Arthur Priest to read. She made such a difference in that young man's life.

Arthur and Dolly are a lovely young couple, devoted to their children, and to all of us at The Home for that matter. The gardeners among the residents here are always giving Arthur advice and seed catalogs these days. Hope he can stand all the help he is getting with his vegetable enterprise.... I wonder if either of Arthur's boys is in Amanda's class.... I don't think so, but I must remember to ask.

7

—

Living Rich

November 24th

It fell to me to confer with our administrator about the date and time for our storytelling night. I found Mr. Detwiler sitting, forlorn, behind his desk, perusing a folder of letters and notes.

"Maybe you're too busy to see me now," I said.

"No, Miss Hattie. I'm always glad to see you—and I'm glad for an interruption to my task. This is my day, once a month, when I go through the Complaints file. You wouldn't believe this file."

"What do they complain about, mostly?"

"The food we serve. It's hard for me to visualize what gorgeous, elegant, tasty, gourmet food some of our people must have been used to! And how shortsighted they were not to realize that they were coming to a place where gourmet food is an impossibility. Our kitchen has to serve not only the 'walking' people, but the ones in the Health Care Center as well. Over two hundred meals, three times a day." He touched the letters again. "Oh, well. It's all a part of this crazy job.... What can I do for you?"

I told him, and we got out a calendar and settled on a date in March.

"I'm glad you're going to tell some more stories," said Mr. D. "That's always the best entertainment of the year. I'm a little dubious, though, about your project this time. I know how much you-all want a swimming pool, and I'd love for you to have one, but I'm afraid it's not to be. At meetings with Management in Charlotte I've been told, more than once, that they cannot afford the expense of even one more small building, which would be a necessity for a pool. I'm afraid you're working toward a lost cause."

"Oh, well—nothing ventured, nothing gained." I went out of his office a little subdued, and left the poor man to his Complaints file. I wouldn't have his job for thrice his salary.

November 25th

I'm being asked to make talks and sign books here, there, and yonder. I can't get to "yonder." Too far. I only drive in the confines of Drayton these days. But if the nice caller wants me to speak at a luncheon in Whoop'n Holler, and will offer to come get me and bring me home, I'll go.

One very nice lady, president of a Friends of the Library group in a county not too far away, phoned and wanted me to be the guest speaker at their annual luncheon. She said she would fetch me and return me. She asked, "What do you charge for your talks?" I was stunned. I never charge *any*thing. I said, "Well...uh..." And she said, "Would $300 and expenses be all right?" I said, "Be *lovely!*" They gave me such a wonderful standing ovation that I felt a little bit mean about taking their money.

People are asking me what I am going to call Novel Number Three. I had decided on "Extra Innings," because goodness knows I'm having them, and because I like baseball. But while I was signing books at a bookstore in Charleston my daughter, who had driven me there, wandered among the shelves and found another book named, alas, *Extra Innings.* I guess I'll have to scratch up something else.

I was going through items that people have sent me, including some funny definitions that appeared in an Elks Club newsletter a few years ago. I don't think the Elks would mind if I put down some of them here.

COUNTRY STYLE MEDICINE

BARIUM	What you do when the patient dies.
BOWEL	A, E, I, O, U, and sometimes Y.
CAUTERIZE	Made contact with her.
ENEMA	Not one of your friends.
GENITAL	Not Jewish.
NITRATES	Cheaper than day rates.
PAP SMEAR	A fatherhood test.
RECTUM	Damn near killed 'em.
TERMINAL ILLNESS	Getting sick at the airport.

URINE	Opposite of "You're out."
VARICOSE	Nearby.
VEIN	Conceited.

Later

Good thought for today:
"It is one of the beautiful compensations of this life that no one can sincerely try to help another without helping himself."—*Charles Dudley Warner.*

December 8th

Amanda called me Sunday night. It was the first time I had heard her voice on the phone. She sounded excited.

After we exchanged greetings, she said, "Guess what! I asked Mrs. Trotter, and she said it was OK."

"OK for what?"

"For you to come to the school and talk to my class."

"Oh, dear. What will I talk about?"

"Well, I want you to bring both of the books you have written and talk about how they came out of your head and got on the paper—and maybe you could say something about what it feels like to live in a place where everybody is old."

"You mean about how we all have hearing aids and eyeglasses and walking canes?"

"Something like that. Only—*you* don't seem that old to me—I just mean—"

"I think I know what you mean, dear. Well, I'll see what I can work up that might interest your classmates. What day?"

"Thursday."

"Thursday, of *this* week?"

"Yes, ma'am. At eleven o'clock. Will you come?"

I promised her I would, but I have misgivings. I don't want to let Amanda down by not measuring up to the buildup she has given me. I can keep her entertained for a while, but she's a dear, polite, responsive child. When I think of thirty faces looking up at me—some of them boys like Melvin, daring me to make them smile.... Oh, me.

December 11th

Well, I went to the school today in trepidation. First of all, I got lost getting there. Drayton is absolutely the worst place to find your way around in. Most of the town was settled 150 years ago and was apparently not meant to survive into the motorized age. The streets wind around and run into each other, and the names change. Fortunately I had left home rather early, because I lost twenty-five minutes getting to the building at 208 Myrtle Avenue. Finally I found my way to Room 3-C. A smiling Mrs. Trotter answered my knock, and Amanda beamed at me from the fourth row.

Mrs. Trotter gave me a chair and asked me to excuse her while she finished handing out some papers. This gave me a chance to look around at the typical classroom, with children's drawings tacked up around the walls, an arithmetic problem printed in large figures on the board, and the smell of chalk and small bodies and bologna sandwiches. I wondered which boy was Melvin.

I never taught school, so I was remembering my own

third-grade days and wondering how in the world I could relate to these little people…. It had been so long since my own children were this small…. *Mrs. Trotter is so young and pretty. They must think I am a thousand years old.*

The teacher asked Amanda to introduce me. She did it in her bright, affectionate way. I thought, *I must not let her down.…* And thank goodness, I don't believe I did. Ten minutes later the children were laughing, and I was finishing my little talk, much relieved. I had dredged up a few memories of my antediluvian school days that they could hardly believe.

Just as I started to talk there was an interruption: an announcement over the public-address system. When it finished I told the children that we had no PA system when I was in school—just a principal with a loud voice. Then I remembered something else that we didn't have: school buses.

"No buses?"

"No. And no cafeterias."

"No cafe*tee*rias?"

"No. I walked to school carrying my books and my little lunch basket that held my muffins and my apple and my hard-boiled egg, all covered by a clean cloth napkin."

I told them about some other things we didn't have, like computers and TVs and movie projectors in the classrooms.

"We managed to learn," I said, "but it was harder. We were not taught to print, just to write." I made them laugh, going to the blackboard and demonstrating the Palmer Method of Writing. (Up-Down, Up-Down, Round, Round, Round We Go.)

I told them that we usually used pencils, but sometimes for special papers the teacher would give out pens, which we had to dip into the inkwells on our desks.

"They didn't have ballpoint pens?" somebody asked.

"No, you dummy," a boy answered. "Ballpoint pens have ink inside of them. But this was *before* that."

"Tell us about your books, Miss Hattie," said Amanda. (I had brought them, as she had asked me to.) "Show them your name on the front."

So I pointed to my name and to the jacket drawings, and opened the books to show some of the illustrations inside. We talked about writing and editing and getting the books to the bookstores and how, all along the way, everyone has to make a profit.

I thanked Mrs. Trotter for letting me come. Amanda hugged me, which made it all worthwhile.

December 15th

We had a little holiday "hen party" yesterday afternoon at Marcia's cottage. There was Christmas punch and also tea, as well as a lovely table of goodies. There were quite a few stories that testified to our "gaiety of soul," even if they weren't, strictly speaking, in the spirit of the season! I'll set some of them down here.

A new man was in the process of moving into a Home (not ours). Down the hall came Louisa, a woman resident who was a quintessential busybody, and also a little more than slightly man-crazy.

"Oh, sir," she said, trotting up to the man. "You're to be

"Tell us about your books, Miss Hattie," said Amanda.

our new neighbor! How nice! Where do you come from?"
She paused to take a breath.

"From prison," he said.

"*Prison?* What did you *do?*"

"I killed my wife. Shot her dead."

Louisa's face lit up. "Oh, then you're *single!*"

I told the story, from long ago, about a very proud, very
poor widow who attended St. Paul's Church in my hometown. When the collection plate was passed she invariably
shook her head, chin up.

One Sunday she was sitting at the end of a row, isolated.
The man passing the plate decided not to bother detouring
to where she was, knowing that it would be a fruitless
journey.

After the service the widow went up to the vestryman in
high dudgeon.

"Why didn't you pass the plate to me?" she demanded.

"Well, I…that is, I thought you wouldn't…well, I just—"

"Young man," she broke in, "you should *always* give me
the privilege of shaking my head."

The biggest laugh of the afternoon came from an anec-
dote about an Episcopal bishop who loved to work in the
gardens and grounds around his home.

One day, the story went, he was working out in his yard
when a large car, driven by a liveried chauffeur, came by and
stopped. A lady in the back seat, complete with lorgnette,
peered out. Then she beckoned to the bishop, who was clad
in work clothes.

"My good man," she said, "do you keep this place up?"

"Yes, madam," he said humbly.

"It's a beautiful place," she said, "but I'll pay you more if you will come and work for me."

The bishop smiled. "But madam," he said, "you don't understand. This is the only place I've ever worked where I have the privilege of sleeping with the lady of the house."

The woman touched the chauffeur on his shoulder and the car took off, fast.

December 17th

Sometimes when people in this town die, they bequeath their books to our library. That is a boon, except to the members of the Library Committee, who have to plow through the books and decide which ones to keep (our space is small) and what to do with the others.

I was going through some dusty volumes in a "bequest" yesterday, and came upon a small, ancient copy—a reprint, not an early edition—of Boswell's *Life of Dr. Johnson*. I took it home, got out my magnifying glass, and had a field day.

I had studied Samuel Johnson briefly in English Lit in college, but I had forgotten how remarkably pithy and up-to-date are the sayings of this man who lived more than two hundred years ago. Many of his maxims apply to our age group. Here are some examples:

"It is a man's own fault, it is from want of use, if his mind grows torpid in old age." (Oh, boy! He hit home there.)

"Everything that enlarges the sphere of human powers, that shows man he can do what he thought he could not do, is valuable."

"He is not only dull himself, but the cause of dullness in others."

"Sir, a woman preaching is like a dog's walking on his hind legs. It is not done well, but you are surprised to find it done at all." (Whooo-eee!)

"Knowledge is of two kinds: we know a subject ourselves, or we know where we can find information upon it."

"There is nothing which has yet been contrived by man by which so much happiness is produced as by a good tavern or inn."

"On clean-shirt day he went abroad and paid visits."

"Oats: a grain which in England is generally given to horses, but in Scotland supports the people."

"I live in a crowd of jollity, not so much to enjoy company as to shun myself."

"Worth seeing? Yes; but not worth *going* to see." (I'm with Dr. Johnson there, in my late days. The going is too hard.)

"Life is very short, and very uncertain; let us spend it as well as we can." (You're so right, Doc.)

Or, as he put it another way, beautifully, "It is better to live rich than to die rich."

December 28th

I spent the holidays with my daughter and her family, which was right and proper, I suppose; but salubrious? No.

I love them all dearly. I call Nancy's husband my favorite son-in-law (which I can do with impunity, since he is my only one), and he calls me his favorite mother-in-law. They couldn't have been nicer to me. *But...*one grandchild had to give up his room to "Nana" and sleep in the den. I hated putting him out. Also, his room is up a thousand steps, it seemed to me, and it is about a thousand steps from the bathroom—a positively dangerous situation.

Those wonderful descendants of mine keep the strangest hours! They start entertaining friends at the oddest times, just as my eyelids start getting heavy.

Their diet is not what I am accustomed to, by any means. There are never any prunes or stewed apples or cream of wheat. There are beautiful steaks, cooked medium-rare on the grill, that my teeth can't handle. There is much pasta and pizza and Mexican food, which came along after "my time."

The grandchildren's radios are constantly blasting "music" that must have been recorded in some padded room in The Bad Place.

I hated to keep pushing the thermostat up, surreptitiously, but they keep their house *so cold*. I was swathed in shawls the whole time like some poor old Siberian grandmother on one of those television travel shows.

So, on reaching it this morning, I wanted to kneel down and kiss the doormat in front of my apartment! "Be it ever so humble...."

December 29th

A CHRISTMAS COMPLAINT

"Shop early" they say, so you buy all your gifts,
And later you feel betrayed
When you see those items advertised
For half the price you paid.

January 5th

Cora's and my mailboxes are close together, in our little post office. We were getting our mail at the same time today, and Cora held up a brown envelope to show me. It had a large window which bore these words:

CORA HUNTER, you have met all the specifi-
cations, and we are PLEASED to tell you that
YOU HAVE DONE IT! You are one of the
LUCKY FINALISTS in our contest!
CORA HUNTER, you are GUARANTEED TO
RECEIVE TEN MILLION DOLLARS
($10,000,000.00)
if you turn in the winning number by February 15th.

The last line was in very small letters.

She tore the envelope open, glanced at the contents, and said, "See, Hattie, they're even asking if I want the money sent to me or to my bank!"

"What's all that other stuff?" I asked. She unfolded a long sheet of catalog names. "You have to enter again? Haven't you already subscribed to a number of their magazines?"

"Oh—a few," she said, a little ruefully, "but this is the final shot. *This* is what counts. And I feel lucky. I'm right up there in the top echelon, they tell me.... Now, let me see. What am I not already getting?"

She opened the list up further. As I walked away I heard her saying, "No, I'm getting that already…and that…and that…."

Oh, dear. Cora is normally such a *sensible* person.

January 6th

Wallace McLean died last night, and I am devastated—not because of him; he was a fine man who had lived a long, happy life and has surely gone to a good reward. I am sad and upset because of his wife, Gracie. Her life has been cut in half—if not in three-quarters.

I have never known such marital devotion as those two had for each other. You never saw one without the other. She is small and frail-looking. They frequently walked around the campus, and always his arm was under hers. If it was raining, his other arm held an umbrella over her. He would take off her raincoat in the cloakroom, straighten her dress, and she would reach up in such an affectionate gesture and smooth down his damp hair.

They did not seem to mind the fact that they had never been blessed with children. They had each other. They did not join in the games at The Home, but played two-handed games together: cribbage and double solitaire. Often they were seen in the library, selecting books to read aloud to each other.

And now, with no warning—no time of preparation—a heart attack has taken Wallace away.

I will have to go to see Gracie, but I dread it. I've heard that he had a sister, who has been sent for. I wonder if Gracie will get any comfort from her—or from the minister—or from *any*body, on this, probably the worst day of her life.

How I hate to think of her coming upon his walking cane, his wallet, his hairbrush.... As one poetic female, Sara Teasdale, put it:

> Things have a terrible permanence
> When people die.

Oh, dear. I remember my Sam's bureau, where he emptied his pockets every night. I can still see the little array that faced me on that dark morning, sixteen years ago: his worn-smooth buckeye, his little four-pronged knife, his keys, his buffalo nickel, and the silver dollar he kept for some sentimental reason (and that I fussed about, because it helped to wear out his pockets)....

There is only one good thing that I can think of this morning: Gracie McLean is fortunate to be living here at FairAcres Home, where there is an amazing amount of heartfelt sympathy and true caring. She will not grieve alone—unless she wants to.

8

Discoveries

January 8th

My hat is off to the admissions officers, or whatever they're called: the people who have to decide on who gets into these retirement homes, and who must be kept out. Disposition *does* count. The authorities want a pleasant atmosphere as much as we do.

But sometimes they make a *big* mistake.

"My cousin Bert is in a home in Georgia," said Edwin yesterday at the table. "He and I were always real close. I went up to see him over the holidays. He's in a beautiful place. It's by a river, where he can walk and fish, and there's even a three-hole golf course; but all he could talk about was the terrible guy in the next room. Bert was in a real tizzy about him. Said he kept the whole hall in a constant uproar, yelling about slights and thefts and being overlooked and being cheated. None of the accusations were true. He just seemed to have to have something to fuss and make trouble about. Somebody who had known him a long time said he had always been that way."

"Lordy! I'm glad we don't have anybody like that here," said Ethel. Heads nodded around the table.

Louly and I exchanged glances but decided not to bring up a certain infamous woman who once accused Arthur of stealing and stirred up a whole mess of trouble. She did not stay long at FairAcres, thankfully. Of the more than two hundred people here now, there is not really a mean trouble-maker in the bunch. We are blessed....

I have about decided that if a man or woman was a rotten child, he or she is a rotten old person. Good training, good schooling, good examples—none of it seems to count with people of the "bad seed" variety.

I remember my mother telling me once that she and her cook, Hannah, were talking, decades ago, about a man they knew, in his sixties, who was rude and selfish and mean. "Same way he wuz born," said Hannah. "I heard folks say he wuz hateful from the day he wuz born. Even *cried* hateful.... I'll tell you sump'm, Miss Annie. People don't change. They jest gits wusser."

January 9th

A male resident came into the dining room this morning and apparently had dressed in too big a hurry. I didn't say anything, and only hoped that nobody else would notice his *dishabille.*

There was a good custom in our family. I had two brothers, and if one of them came into a room and somebody in the family said quietly, "*X, Y, Z,*" he knew what it meant: "Xamine Your Zipper."

That was a great and timely signal, especially if company was present. Maybe we should have some signals like that here.

January 11th

Christine and I arranged for Gracie McLean to go with us to church this morning, and all afternoon I have been remembering the words to a hymn we sang:

> Drop thy still dews of quietness
> 'Til all our strivings cease;
> Take from our souls the strain and stress
> And let our ordered lives confess
> The beauty of thy peace.

Thank you, Mr. John Greenleaf Whittier (you of the pretty and poetic name) for those graceful lines. Don't tell *me* the old hymns aren't more beautiful and meaningful than most of those being turned out today.

Gracie is doing better than I expected. We all went out to lunch together, and by the time we parted company, she was recalling fond memories of Wallace, with some mist in her eyes, but with a soft smile.

January 12th

One of our number told me something funny today. He said he was driving through North Carolina a few years ago, and he stopped at a roadside restaurant in a town with an odd name: Fuquay Varina.

When the waitress came to take his order, he said to her, "Please do me a favor. Tell me how to pronounce the name of this place."

The waitress smiled and said, "I'll be glad to." Bending down close to his ear, she said, very clearly, "It's HAR-DEE's."

January 15th

A woman (I'll call her Mary) was visiting our Home yesterday. I think she had some business in the front office, and somebody deposited her at our table to eat lunch. She was cheerful and agreeable and we all liked her immediately, but the poor thing had a Figure Fault with a capital *F*.

Before our two male table companions arrived, Gusta whispered to me, "Did you ever see such boobs? When she sits down she holds 'em in her lap!"

Mary must have seen somebody at the table looking at her chest area. She grinned and said, "I know I'm a sight. I seem to defeat the most uplifting bra. You see, I nursed four babies, and the last one wouldn't wean. He would *not* take a bottle. I nursed him till he was two years old. I couldn't let him starve! He'd stand up by my low rocking chair and help himself—first on one side and then he'd walk around to the other."

By this time we were in stitches. She smiled and said, "He's a big, strong man now. Had a good start." She took another helping of potatoes and smiled good-naturedly. "When I see my bare figure in the bathroom mirror, all I can think about are those native women in *National Geographic* magazines. I guess there aren't any baby bottles in many parts of the world."

"I guess not," somebody said. I looked around uneasily, but our two men were not yet in sight, thank goodness.

Mary laughed, remembering something. "The funniest thing was when my husband and I went to a fancy dinner party, and halfway through the dinner I saw him looking down the table at me (we were sitting far apart) and making signs. I looked down. One bra strap must have broken. My left bosom had gone southward about six inches. I had on a tight, satin dress, and you can imagine what the discrepancy looked like." She made graphic gestures with her hands. "All I could do was feign a bad coughing spell. Some guests may have wondered why I held the napkin over my bosom instead of my mouth. Anyway, I slipped out to the powder room and got that left side jerked back up and fastened good. Got back in time for dessert!"

Perhaps we'll have to come up with signals for ladies' as well as gentlemen's problems of attire.

January 16th

I haven't heard from Amanda Pate since before Christmas. She and others in the class wrote after my visit, plus she and I exchanged Christmas cards. But I'm getting a bit worried and afraid she might be sick. I miss her dear little weekly notes—I miss hearing about Melvin's mischief. If I don't get a note soon I will call Mrs. Trotter.

January 17th

While I was lying in the tub this morning, meditating and occasionally washing, suddenly my new cake of Ivory soap got away from me. There was a scramble and a frantic hunt, and I got madder by the minute. This was *Ivory*. It should *float*. It has floated all my life. The first ad I ever remember reading claimed, "It floats." The friendly little white cake has never failed to pop to the surface in all these years—but it failed me now. It sank.

Oh, dear! Does *every*thing have to change? They've creamed up the soap. It's better for my skin, they say. I think it has lost more than it has gained. I feel like suing somebody.

Speaking of ablutions: most of my friends take showers. That's their privilege, but I think they're missing a lot. I get some of my best thinking done as I lie still in the warm, scented water. It's easier than showering. I just let the soaking do most of the work while I settle, in my mind, the affairs of nations and of things nearer home.

Later

I like crossword puzzles. I buy paperback books of them—the kind of books that have answers in the back for those who like to cheat. I try hard not to look at the answers, but many times I can not finish the puzzle without cheating.

A clue in the puzzle I worked today was: "What a thanatomaniac likes to read." Believe it or not, I knew the answer: O-B-I-T-S. I think having studied the poem "Thanatopsis" in high school may have helped me to know that a thanatomaniac is someone who has an extraordinary interest in death.

I try not to think too much about my death; but at my great age, the specter looms, willy-nilly.

It is then that I recall the wonderful words that Thomas Wolfe wrote at the end of *You Can't Go Home Again.*

> Something has spoken to me in the night…and told me that I shall die, I know not where. Saying: "[Death is] to lose the earth you know, for greater knowing; to lose the life you have, for greater life; to leave the friends you loved, for greater loving; to find a land more kind than home, more large than earth—"

To add any comment of mine, after those words, would be like "holding a farthing candle to the sun."

January 18th

This raw and wintry day was perfect for staying inside, keeping warm, and remembering.

When my late husband was about fourteen and fifteen, he attended a prep school in Bell Buckle, Tennessee: The Webb School. In later years I would tease Sam and say that he must have been the town's "Peck's Bad Boy," to have been sent so far, to such a strict place. But he said his parents thought it would be good for him to learn some Latin and Greek, neither of which was taught in his small-town high school.

Webb School was (and still is) famous for Latin, Greek, and discipline. If you were asked a question and failed it, you went to the foot of the class, literally; and Sam told me about dire punishments for staying too long at the class's foot.

He could recite rules of Latin grammar *ad nauseum,* and whole paragraphs of Virgil's *Aeneid.* I'm not sure that proved of much use in his career (he owned and operated a trucking line), but maybe the discipline had an effect.

During his first weeks at the school, Sam had a physical problem. Too much starchy food, probably, and not enough fruit, like figs and prunes. He said he kept thinking of the phrase, "That makes the cheese more binding." He felt completely bound, and he didn't even have any of the Castoria that his mother would have given him.

Finally he felt compelled to go to the school's doctor, a country-type practitioner who gave Sam no time and no sympathy—not even a dose of Castoria. He waved him out of the office after one minute, saying, "Let Nature take its course, son. Go on…jest keep a-eatin', son. Jest keep a-eatin'."

The doctor proved to be right, and the phrase "Jest keep a-eatin'" passed down in the family. Not very elegant, but sensible.

Later

I found these lines I had copied in an old notebook. I think they were written by Ralph Waldo Emerson.

Some of your hurts you have cured
And the sharpest you still have survived,
But what torments of grief you have endured
From evils which never arrived!

And two more sagacious lines from the same gentleman's pen:

The music that can deepest reach
And cure all ills, is cordial speech.

January 25th

I telephoned Mrs. Trotter, Amanda's teacher, at her home this afternoon, and asked her if Amanda was sick.

"No," she said, "but she hasn't seemed to be her bubbly self lately. I've been wondering if something was wrong."

"Can you find out?"

"I'll try," she said. "I'll call you back if I learn anything."

Sure enough, she called tonight with disturbing news.

"Mrs. McNair? I talked to Sarah Finletter. She's best friends with Tallulah Pate, Amanda's mother. Sarah's worried about the whole family. Here's the story: Terry Pate, the father, had a fine job at the Charleston Naval Base for years. But, as you know, that base was closed by the government. Most of the people who worked there have managed to find other jobs by now, but not Terry. For one thing, his work was specialized—something to do with nuclear submarines, I believe—the kind of job that doesn't transfer easily. Also, Terry's a very reserved person. Not the kind to push himself; so he hasn't been able to find work. Their very nice house has a For Sale sign in the yard. Sarah thinks it was when that sign went up that Amanda went into a slump."

"What are they living on, do you know?"

"It seems that Tallulah has a part-time job, and Terry is caning chairs for people in his workshop."

I thanked Mrs. Trotter and hung up, worried. That dear, sensitive child, Amanda—it hurt me that she was troubled and embarrassed.... What is that sound I'm hearing? I think it must be my busybody genes. They're beginning to stir!

January 26th

I went to the Maintenance Department today and asked Arthur Priest if there were any cane-bottomed chairs or benches in The Home that needed fixing. I told him briefly about my little friend's father being out of a job. Arthur has a good heart, and responded as I knew he would.

"Let's take a look, Miss Hattie. I think I remember one chair with a break in the seat."

As we walked down the hall we talked about his family— his own three adorable children, and his little foster sons, Jamie and Jeffrey—the ones that we "inmates" had been so interested in. It seemed they were all flourishing.

"Sometimes they're too noisy, and Kudzu Kottage sounds like a zoo—but most of the time it's great. I like being Big Daddy, and Dollie likes her job too. She's not working at the school anymore, you know. She bakes pies and cakes for several places around town, which allows her to stay busy at home, and happy." That was good to hear.

Soon we reached the small parlor, and sure enough there in the corner was a chair with a hole in the middle of its cane seat.

"I've been meaning to do something about this before somebody like Mr. Comstock sits on it," said Arthur, in a whisper. (Mr. Comstock has a vast posterior.)

I told Arthur I would help out The Home by paying for the repair. He seemed pleased, and carried the chair to my car.

After I got back to my apartment, I called Mr. Pate and arranged to take the chair to him in the morning and got directions for finding the house.

January 27th

When I made my way to 112 Greenway Street today, I was struck by the white clapboard house, obviously old and beautifully restored. No wonder Amanda loved it. The house and grounds had a settled-in, cared-for look. Her dog Buster gave a friendly bark and wagged his tail as he came toward me. I could see her cat asleep in a sunny window. No wonder my little friend hated the large For Sale sign that stood in a corner of the yard.

I knew that Amanda was at school, so instead of going to the house I headed for the small building on the back of the lot, where Mr. Pate had told me he would be. I could hear the sound of an electric saw, and I had to knock twice before he heard me and came to the door.

"Mrs. McNair?"

"Yes, Mr. Pate, I'm Harriet McNair, your daughter's pen pal."

"Please come in. I've heard Manda talk a lot about you."

He was a pleasant looking man, but his voice was so low I had to strain to hear him. I asked if he would have time to do the caning for me. He said he would, and he went out to the street to get the chair out of my car.

This gave me a chance to look around his neat workshop. I was surprised at the amount of woodworking machinery he had, for a "caner"—and then I saw them: three pieces of furniture in a corner. There was a chest of drawers that appeared to be made of warm cherry wood and a table of gleaming walnut, but it was a small desk—a "lady's desk" it had to be—that grabbed my attention. It was simple but elegant, and was made of wood of a very light hue—cream colored—with a dark trim. Most unusual. I was enthralled.

When he came back in I was touching the desk. "What is this wood?" I asked.

"It's curly maple. The trim is ebony."

The delicate trim set off a row of pigeon holes, and below that were four tiny drawers. The drawer pulls were also made of ebony, as were the pulls on the two larger drawers below the writing surface. The slant-top was down. Everything was open, airy, lovely.

I ran my fingers across the pediment, fashioned from the same creamy wood. Its lacy design finished off the piece to perfection. I am no furniture connoisseur, but I knew that I was looking at real artistry here. In front of it stood a slender chair, also of curly maple, just exactly the right size and style to go with the desk.

"Is this desk for sale? And the chair?" I asked.

"Yes, ma'am.... I hate to tell you the price. I had a time getting the two woods I wanted, and I spent many an hour making them. I have to ask $500 for the desk, and $100 for the chair."

"I don't blame you. They are beautiful pieces, and they will fit perfectly in my bedroom. I'd like to buy them."

I am not usually an impulsive buyer, but this time I didn't even hesitate. I wrote him a check for the desk and the chair and for the caning, and he promised to deliver my purchases along with the recaned chair.

"I have a neighbor who has a pickup truck, and he'll help me.... Mrs. McNair, this desk is a special piece to me. I designed it and worked hard on it. I'm real glad for you to have it. You've been nice to my daughter."

"And that has been a joy," I told him. "She's a very dear child." I wanted to say more, to ask about her being depressed, but decided it would be best not to get too personal. Not yet, anyway.

"I'll call you as soon as I'm ready to bring everything out," said Mr. Pate as I opened the door to leave. "And thank you, ma'am."

"Thank *you*," I said heartily. I got in my car feeling a rare elation. My two books are selling well, and until now I have not given myself a present out of the royalties. As I drove away a lovely thought hit me. I would bequeath the desk to Amanda! She had no doubt seen her father working on it. It would have meaning for her.... I think I will let her father know what I intend. That will make it easier for him

I am no furniture connoisseur, but I knew
that I was looking at real artistry here.

to part with it. I could tell that he has a real affection for the little set.

Later

I'm trying to accomplish something that has a sad urgency about it. I love to play the piano, and I was pleased to be able to get my spinet into the apartment here. But, alas, retina trouble is making it harder every day for me to read the music. I am now trying with all my might to memorize my favorite numbers before the time comes when I can't distinguish the tiny notes.

I'm working on Chopin's "Raindrop Prelude" and his Nocturne in E-flat, a Mozart Minuet, Tchaikovsky's "Chanson Triste," Massenet's "Elegie" and "Meditation," and even a Bach Invention. They are all fairly easy selections, with melodies that please my soul. Now if I can just hold them in my poor old mind and fingers....

By the way, Dear Diary, I'd like to set something straight. Since writing in here about my new Ivory Soap cake sinking, I have learned that, whereas Messrs. Proctor and Gamble have added a new line of Ivory that is so creamy and heavy that it sinks, they do *still* make the good little cakes that have floated since my childhood—and that are "99 and 44/100%" pure. Thank goodness. I'll just have to shop more carefully. (And I won't worry about the 56/100% that's not pure.)

9

—

More Revelations

January 28th

Today some of us (all females) got to talking about our mothers—about the clothes they wore.

"How did they stand those corsets and 'corset covers'—camisoles?—in hot weather? With no air-conditioning?" Mary wondered.

"Our mothers must've been made of stronger stuff," somebody said. "When Mama's corset wore out she gave my brother and me the stays to play with. We used them as weapons."

"And the long, long hair they had to wash and tend to!" remembered Chris. "My mother brushed her hair every night—a hundred strokes—and then plaited it. I can see that long braid now, hanging down the back of her white cambric nightgown."

Several people nodded. It was a common memory. A dear one.

"Did your mothers have a 'bureau set'? Sometimes called a 'vanity set'?" asked Elsie. Several people nodded. "My mother's set was crystal trimmed with silver. *Fancy.* Let's see, there was a tray, and on it...there were the mirror, the comb and brush, the nail file, the shoe-button hook—what else?"

"Mama's set had a nail buffer," I remembered.

"And a glove hook," someone contributed, "for buttoning those tiny buttons on gloves!"

"You all have missed one of the main pieces," said Christine. "That was a little crystal bowl with a silver top. I think they called it a 'hair-receiver.' They saved the hair that came out of the comb and put it in the bowl."

"Why in the world did they save that?" asked Elsie.

"When you had enough strands of hair saved you had a 'rat' made out of them. That was a coil of hair that you could use on top of your head, or to make the bun bigger on the back of your neck."

"Think of a bun on the back of your neck—in South Carolina heat, with no air-conditioning!" I looked around at us. Every single head had a short, curled, cool hairdo. So much more comfortable. And yet...remembering how very feminine my mother had looked in her ruffled nightgown and her long braid of sweet-smelling hair...I wonder if we have sacrificed something to comfort and convenience.

Musing.

I'm smiling over a memory.

When my daughter got married and had children, she wanted to take them to the doctor who had treated her as a child, Dr. Lanes, whom she remembered as being gentle and kind.

In the meantime he had specialized in pediatrics, and moved his practice to Charleston. It made trips to the doctor a little harder, but she followed him. Her son and daughter loved him.

When her son Eric was a senior at the College of Charleston he developed an ailment—his first sickness in years. He got in his low-down sports car and drove to the office of Dr. Lanes, the only doctor he had ever known. The waiting room was full of mothers and babies—some of the mothers younger than he. They must have looked askance at the 180-pound patient with a black mustache.

He held his ground, got treated, and then was told by the nurse, kindly, that maybe he'd better find another doctor.

He went out shrugging and wondering why everything had to change.

January 29th

Oh-oh. Trouble with the left knee—the operated-on one. The stainless steel joint is wobbling.

I went to see my knee doctor, and called attention politely to the warranty he gave me six months ago: thirty years on the parts, nothing on the labor.

He had the civility to blush a little, but quickly blamed Nature and my anatomy. He said my muscles are not strong enough to hold the appliance in place, and of course he's right. So I am now on a delightful regimen of exercises, three times a day, and I have to wear a brace that pinches and squeezes and shows below my skirt, and takes five hurting minutes to put on and take off.

I've often wondered how old Robert Browning was when he wrote:

> Grow old along with me!
> The best is yet to be,
> The last of life, for which the first was made.

Fifty, maybe? When he still had his decent teeth and eyes and ears, his good knees, and a strong bladder? And still had his loved ones and his good friends?

Whoever said, "Old age is not for sissies" must have been in his or her seventies or eighties. Not as flowery as Mr. Browning, but much more "on the ball."

Later

I remember an old spiritual:

> Nobody knows the trouble I've seen,
> Nobody knows but Jesus.

Well, if you live in a home for the elderly, you're with people who have seen trouble in varying degrees, and who are pretty sure they'll see more before "That Great Gittin'-Up Mornin.'"

But most of them refuse to let that thought get them down or daunt their spirits. And they are *so* ready and eager to laugh. I've been delighted to learn that I've made many of them laugh with my two little books.

I was afraid some of them, in reading about what I call The Home, might see resemblances to real people and be offended. But as far as I can find out, this has not happened. They seem really pleased about the success of the books, and they're eager to supply me with funny "overheards." Bless their hearts! As the old song says, I love "those dear hearts and gentle people" that live in my retirement home. Trouble is, I want them *all* to keep *on* living, as long as I do.

That reminds me of an incident years ago when my youngest granddaughter, sitting in my lap, looked up at me and said, "Nana, how old are you?"

I said, "Let's put it this way, I'm as young as I feel, and as old as I look."

She turned her eyes up to my face and said, "*That* old?"

Oh, dear.

January 30th

My eavesdropping paid off today. Paul and Curtis were in rare form, and I was listening with all my might.

Paul said, "Got any good stories, Curt?"

Curtis said, "Not a one worth waggin' my tongue over. You?"

"Well," said Paul, "I remember a crazy thing.... Let me see.... Oh, yes. There was a fellow named Hencil who boarded an airplane and sat down by a woman. He took a quick look and saw that she was the most beautiful female he had ever seen. It was going to be a short trip. He *had* to get to know her, and he had to work fast. So he turned to her and said, 'Excuse me, ma'am, but what kind of men do you like best?' The woman was a mite startled. She thought for a few seconds while he looked at her eagerly, and then she said, 'Well, let's see.... I like Indians—Native Americans, I mean—and I like strong Jewish men. But I think best of all I just like good old boys.... By the way, sir, what is your name?'

"Quick as a flash Hencil said, 'My name is Geronimo Steinberg, but most people just call me Bubba.'"

Paul and Curtis thigh-slapped over that one. After a while Curtis said, "Speakin' of names, you 'bout got your entries lined up for the car-namin' contest?"

"I've got a pretty good list. Now I've got to narrow it down to three."

"I still vote for Stallion," said Curtis. "Or maybe Studmobile, which you could cut down to Studly."

They both laughed again.

After a minute, Paul said, "I've noticed they've given some of the newer cars the names of places: Seville, Tahoe, Riviera, Montana."

"Well, hey!" said Curtis. "That opens lots of new ground! Why, right here in South Carolina we've got some towns with great names you could use, like Pomaria and Round O and Coosawhatchie and Ninety-Six."

Paul joined in the fun. "Somewhere I've got a list of town

names I've liked. I remember a few of them: Tuckahoe, Pigstown, Provo, Thunderhawk, Equinunk—"

"Wow," said Curtis, "the possibilities are endless!"

Names have always interested me, especially when they get twisted around into a humorous bungle. I recall an elderly cousin of mine who had a way of "improving" on the nomenclature of things. That nice bush with the odd name: Pittosporum? I think that's the right spelling. Anyway, Cousin Boo always called it "spitty-sporum." And that bush called Elæagnus—she always called it "Ailing Agnes."

A similar "improvement" occurred not too long ago when I stopped to admire an arrangement of flowers on a table in the entrance hall.

"Those tulips are gorgeous!" I said aloud to myself. "And that lovely, lacy white stuff mixed in—what do they call it?" I mused.

"Pyorrhea," came the answer from a lady walking by. Spirea will now always have that name to me.

Oh, I heard another good story about an elderly woman who made an appointment with an attorney.

As she sat down in front of his desk, he asked how he might help her.

"I want to file for a divorce."

The lawyer was a little taken aback. "Ma'am, may I ask how old you are, and how long you've been married?"

"I am eighty-three, and I've been married for sixty-two

years. To the same man."

"May I ask why you want a divorce, ma'am?"

"I'll tell you why," she said. "Enough is enough."

February 2nd

Ethel is good about pushing people about in wheelchairs. She makes a point of seeing that all the wheelchair people get transported to the chapel for Sunday morning service.

Yesterday she pushed Mr. Crowder, a quiet man who may have had a lot of marbles at one time but retains few of them now.

When the service was over Ethel went up to the front and divided the lovely bouquet of daisies among several wheelchair people, including Mr. Crowder. As Ethel pushed him back to his room she was busy speaking to all the people they passed. When she unlocked his door and turned to push him through, she was aghast to see that he was holding only stems.

"Did you *eat* the daisies?" she asked.

"Yes, and they were delicious!" Mr. Crowder responded, smiling.

Bill Nixon swears this is true. He said his grandfather bought a hearing aid—an almost invisible one—and he didn't tell anybody about it.

Bill said, "He just sat around listening—and then he changed his will!"

February 3rd

Somebody said at lunch today, "I really wonder what happened to that old man's portrait. Do you suppose Management has any clues?"

Nobody seemed to think so.

I'm sure there are two people who could shed some light on the subject. Enough time has passed now that I decided to try the direct approach and cornered my quarry in a quiet part of the dining room after most people had left. I will not call their names—not even to you, Dear Diary. Somebody might happen to read this.

We chatted a while. Finally I plucked up my nerve and confronted them boldly. "Where is Mr. Asa Purifoy?" I asked.

"What?"

"Where is Mr. Purifoy—his likeness, that is?"

"How would we know?" they replied almost in unison.

"You know. I'm sure of it." If I had had any doubts, they were gone now. Those two looked like boys who had been caught with their hands in the cookie jar. "You might as well tell me now. I won't give you any peace until you do."

"Hattie, can we trust you not to go to Headquarters and get us into a mess?"

"Why would I do that? I was just as glad to get rid of that ugly face as anybody. I won't make any trouble. I promise, on my Girl Scout honor."

So they told me.

They had checked out the night watchman's schedule. They learned that he made a complete round of the campus at 3:00 A.M., going behind all the cottages. So on that rainy night the two men slipped into the dining room at three o'clock, carrying only a small flashlight. They mounted two chairs in front of the mantel and got the portrait down.

"We huffed and puffed," said Mr. X. "Ole Pukey Face was heavy. We nearly dropped the old goat a couple of times, but with main force and cussedness we managed to get him to the chapel."

"The *chapel?*"

"That's right," said Mr. Y. "We knew Housekeeping would find the durn thing if we put it under a bed or in a closet. We didn't have the strength to dig a hole and bury it outside—and besides, we were afraid somebody might see us. We thought about it long and hard. My pal here remembered that there's a curtained-off place in the back of the chapel that might do. That inside entrance was a help, because it was raining."

Suddenly I remembered. The funds to build a beautiful chapel were left to our Home about five years ago in the will of a beloved resident, Suzannah Guthrie. She had plans drawn before she died, and the plans called for a choir loft in the back of the sanctuary. But this item was left to the last, and the money gave out before stairs could be built and the loft finished. A place was found in the front of the chapel for the choir, and the unfinished place upstairs in the back, with a ladder leading up to it, was hidden by a heavy velvet curtain. That curtain had evidently caught our culprits' eyes. Nobody ever went behind it.

"We got behind the curtain all right, but we had a little trouble gettin' the old boy up that ladder," said Mr. X. "We weren't real sure there was a floor up there; but there was, and Mr. P's likeness is resting on it. In peace, we hope."

Mr. Y chuckled. "We said a few words that hadn't been heard in *that* place before, eh, chum? I don't know if you'd call us 'older but wiser.' I guess we're more like 'older but wilder'!" They both grinned sheepishly.

Well, sir! Who would ever have thought it! I will probably have trouble getting to sleep tonight. My mind is full of the derring-do of two aging paladins. I had to admire their spunk. Oh, how I pray their secret will not be found out!

February 4th

Sure enough, sleep eluded me last night. I finally got so desperate that I decided to organize some of my tax information. I found a poem I wrote a few years ago on a blue day in April. The sentiments still hold.

IN THE SPRING AN OLDSTER'S FANCY
HEAVILY TURNS TO THOUGHTS OF
COMPUTERS IN CHAMBLEE, GEORGIA
or
MANY HAPPY RETURNS

I'm busy gathering figures and facts
For the (cuss deleted) income tax.
It's a sickening chore. It's a pain in the neck.
And the worst part's coming: writing the check.

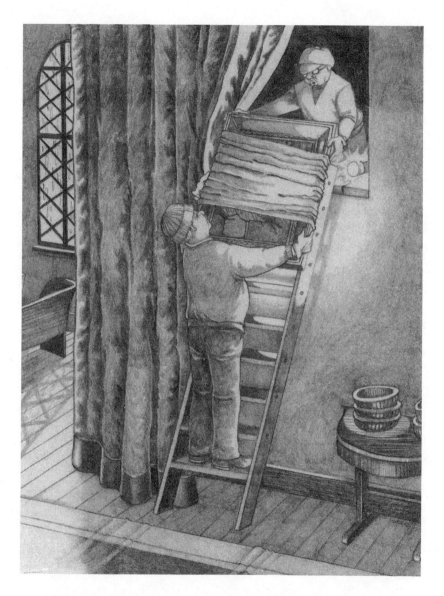

*"We got behind the curtain all right, but we had a
little trouble gettin' the old boy up that ladder."*

The beautiful springtime goes to waste
While I hunt receipts and things misplaced,
And study the tortuous instructions
To try to dig out a few deductions.

I don't mind paying my proper share,
But so much about it isn't fair,
And my money's wasted. It's all a mess.
A pox on Uncle and his IRS!

February 5th

Mr. Pate and his neighbor brought the desk and chair to my apartment today. I saw him rub his fingers affectionately over the smooth top. He hated to let it go.

I told him at once about my plan to leave the desk and chair to Amanda. His smile was my reward.

"Mrs. McNair, that's wonderful of you! Manda will be as pleased as I am." He shook my hand warmly, got directions for where to leave the mended chair, and left.

I called Retta and told her I had something very special to show her. Curious about my excitement, she rushed right over.

"Hattie! It's *beautiful!*" she proclaimed, as soon as she saw my prize. (Retta's first husband owned a furniture factory in High Point, North Carolina, and she knows a lot about fine woods and what can be done with them.) "Where did you find it? How much did you pay for it?"

When I told her the amount she raised her eyebrows. Pulling out the tiny drawers, touching the fancy pediment, she shook her head. "It would've been a steal at twice the price."

"Really?" I could hardly believe it; but then, I haven't bought much furniture lately.

"No doubt about it. This man is a gifted artisan.... You say Mr. Pate designed it and made every bit of it himself?"

"Every bit," I told her.

"The chair, too?"

"Oh, yes. He has a workshop in his backyard." I told her about how Mr. Pate lost his Navy Yard job, and how he is living mostly on what he can earn caning chairs.

"He shouldn't just be doing caning when he can turn out a work of art like this.... I want Sidney to see this pretty thing...and I'll tell you what I'm going to do, Hattie. I'm going to call up Herb Murphree in High Point. He's still in the furniture business in a big way, and he was a good friend of Hal's and mine. He has his own factory. I think he will want to see this desk and meet its maker."

Well, sir! It seems, Dear Diary, that I have embarked again on what might be called Busybody Waters! I hope I'm not stirring up a gale.

10

Partings

February 9th

Retta must have given Mr. Murphree an earful over the phone, because here he was *this morning* in my bedroom, down on his knees, examining my little desk from every angle, with a magnifying glass!

Retta and I watched quietly as he got up and stood back a little and sort of measured with his hands.

"It's perfect!" he said. "Light. Airy. Frenchy. We don't have enough of those qualities in American furniture."

("Frenchy." That was the adjective, or at least the description, I'd been searching my mind for.)

"Are you at all interested in selling this desk, Mrs. McNair? I will give you $1,000 for it."

My eyes popped. Double what I paid for it!

"No, thank you. It has settled down nicely in my room …and," I explained, "I have decided to bequeath both pieces back to Amanda. As you can see, I've already put my best notepaper in the drawers."

"So I see." He was now examining the graceful little chair. "Retta, I want to meet this man. Take me to him. If he can turn out something this exquisite in an amateur workshop, think what he could do with state-of-the-art equipment!"

"Come on, Hattie," said Retta. "You know where he lives."

Later

What excitement! Mr. Murphree met Terry Pate, watched him work on a stool he was making, examined the finished pieces in the corner, and made him an offer of a job in High Point! I wasn't close enough to hear the particulars, but I saw Mr. Pate's face light up.

Suddenly I had a distressing thought about my little friend: Amanda is not going to want to leave this, the beloved home of her entire life. Oh, dear. Hattie, maybe you have overstepped…. And then I looked at her father again. He was beaming. He would have a new chance, in work that he liked to do…. Amanda would just be obliged to adjust…. I believe she can do it…. I have a feeling that seeing her father depressed has been a big part of her trouble. Now if she sees him happy, maybe she can stand the move…. I'll have to pray about it.

February 10th

I ran into Marcia in the lobby today. She took me by the arm and said, "I want to tell you something funny. Will you come into the parlor a minute?"

"I'd follow you all the way downtown to hear something funny. This has not been the best of days."

"Well, this is choice, I think," said Marcia as we settled into a pair of wing chairs. "You may know that Geneva has been after me for weeks to take her to a certain store in Charleston, the Easy Spirit Shoe Store. So I took her today.

"We walked in. The poor innocent clerk walked up to us, and Geneva confronted him, announcing her request loudly.

"'I want to try on a pair of those Street Walker shoes I've been hearing about,' she said, with her usual confidence.

"The clerk glanced at me, raised his eyebrows, and seated us, with a look that said, 'Now I've heard everything.' I could have gone through the floor.

"Well, she bought a pair of the shoes, and as the clerk was packaging them he said, 'I think you will find these are very nice Street Walker shoes, ma'am.' And he winked at me."

Giggling, I asked, "How in the world could Neva mix up Easy Spirit and Street Walker?"

"I don't know, but she did, and she made that shoe clerk's day," said Marcia.

She had made mine brighter, too.

February 11th

What a dream I had early this morning! I was glad to wake up.

I dreamed that some of us from The Home were on a trip to...somewhere...on a large Greyhound bus. Sitting there quietly in my bus seat I looked down and discovered that I had put on a long, long slip with a ruffle on the bottom (meant to go with an evening dress) under a short-skirted dress. I was mortified. The slip was on an elastic band, so I was able to squirm out of it. I found a bag somewhere and put the slip in it. I had on a thin dress, and with no slip I soon got cold in the air-conditioned bus. And I worried that people would see right through my dress.

The bus stopped at a large restaurant for lunch. During the short stop, I, of course, went to the restroom twice. (That part of the dream was completely natural.) The second time I stayed too long, and when I came out the bus had gone. I stood there on the sidewalk, forlorn and bewildered, and even grieving that I had left my nice, long slip in a bag on the bus that had departed for Who-Knows-Where!

I did not eat pork for supper last night, nor any highly spiced food that might have caused my stomach to send garbled messages to the neurons (or whatever) in my brain. I had not watched anything wild and disturbing on TV during the evening. I had slept quietly, I think, until just before waking up. Why did I then board a bus for a trip that left me wretched on waking, and for hours afterward?

I once heard somebody say, "I think bad dreams are a

kind of punishment." It's disturbing. Maybe I had better straighten up and fly right-er. I know there's plenty of room for improvement.

Later...still musing

I still have that slip, but I haven't worn it or thought about it for years. Why did it pop into my sleeping mind, and make me miserable? I wonder what Dr. Freud would have said.

February 12th

I went into the library this morning and saw Paul at his usual table, with notebook and thesaurus. He was surrounded by residents giving him what they considered hot suggestions for car names. Our whole "student body" is highly interested in Paul's entry into the contest.

Elsie said, "How about Venture?"

"That's a possibility," said Paul, and wrote it down.

"Paul, you know you couldn't find a better name than Paramount," stated Cecil.

"That's a good one, Cecil, but it's too long. There's no rule, but I've heard that they like names with no more than seven or eight letters. They fit the name-plates better."

Cecil counted out the letters on his fingers. "N-E-W Y-O-R-K-E-R...P-A-R-K A-V-E-N-U-E.... They're longer than Paramount."

"I know it," said Paul, "but those models are older. I wanted to send in Sovereign, but I think it's too long."

"Well, I'll tell you what," said Cecil. "Why don't you just

name it Tomcat and be done with it? Something that prowls, and can take off scalded!"

Everyone laughed, and Cecil and the others walked away. Paul winked at me and motioned me over.

"Tomcat might be good, at that.... What do you think of this list, Hattie?"

I read what he had written down today: "Supreme, Paragon, Rival, Ultra, Orion, Monarch, Champion, Corsair, Resolve."

"I like all of them except Resolve. Somehow, to me, that just doesn't quite fit the bill."

"Then I shall resolve to take it off the list." He smiled. "What do you think of Orion?"

"I like it. One of the better-known constellations. Shining and brilliant. I *like* it."

"Then maybe it will be one of the three names I'll send in." He frowned. "You know something, Hattie? I'm so out of touch, it may be that some of these names"—he picked up his list—"are already in use. I'd better get out on the road and start watching cars."

I shook my head. "They go too fast for me to read the names, if my eyes could reach that far."

"I know. We labor under handicaps, don't we?" From the back of his notebook he pulled out the very official-looking entry blank that National Motors had sent, at his request. "Let's see. According to this, my entries have to arrive in New York by a week from Monday. That doesn't give me much more time. Actually, I'll be glad when this foolishness is over. It's probably a pure waste of time. But then, what better do I have to spend my stellar intellect on?... Hey, that's an idea!" He grabbed his pen and added Stellar to his list.

February 13th

I spent this frigid February day keeping warm and cozy and "scrolling through"—I think that's the right computer term I hear my grands using—various memories that I might offer for our storytelling event.

The first possibility that came to mind was a true story. I wouldn't have believed this really happened, except that I knew the young woman, back in my hometown, and I knew that she had the nerve to do and say exactly what it pleased her to do and say, no matter how outrageous.

Millie was pregnant, and went to the doctor for her third checkup. She sat down in the waiting room and picked up an old magazine. She was in the midst of reading a good story when the nurse called her name and led her to a tiny, cold, featureless, bookless cubicle, telling her to take off everything from her waist down, get up on the table, and cover up with the sheet.

Millie waited and waited. Still no doctor. She got so tired and bored with waiting that she decided to have her revenge. When she finally heard the doctor opening the door she pulled the sheet over her head and yelled, "Guess who?!"

It happened! But it's not quite right for me to tell, not in mixed company.

This little tale might strike some as being sacrilegious. It gave me a laugh, however, and might be worth passing on.

A rather spoiled boy was giving his mother and father lots of trouble. The first-grade teacher sent bad reports: "He's disruptive, he fights, he pays no attention."

The parents employed every punishment they knew of, to no avail. He made it to the second grade, but the reports were just as bad.

Finally, when he was in the third grade, the parents in desperation took him out of the public school and entered him in a private Catholic school.

At once his grades improved. The reports sent home were excellent. The father said, "Son, this is wonderful. I'm proud of you. What happened?"

"Well, I'll tell you, Dad. The very first day, when I saw that big picture on the wall of the fellow they had nailed to the plus sign, I figured I'd better get with it."

Whooo-eee. I hope that didn't happen. I'd hate to think of any third-grader not knowing that was Jesus on the cross. Let's see…perhaps I could read this piece, sent to me by some kind person. It's called "Retirement from a Child's View." It seems that after Christmas vacation, a teacher asked her young pupils how they spent their holidays. One small boy wrote the following:

> We spent Christmas with Grandma and Grandpa. They used to live here in a big brick house, but Grandpa got retarded and they moved to Florida. We went to see them. They live in a place with a lot of other retarded people. They ride on big three-wheeled tricycles, and they

all wear name tags because they don't know who they are.

They go to a building called a wrecked hall, but if it was wrecked they got it fixed because it is all right now. They play games and do exercises there, but they don't do them very good.

There is a swimming pool there, outside. They go into it and just stand there with their hats on. I guess they don't know how to swim.

As you go into their park, there is a dollhouse with a little man sitting in it. He watches all day so they can't get out without him seeing them. When they can sneak out they go to the beach and pick up shells they think are dollars.

My Grandma says Grandpa worked all his life and earned his retardment. I wish they would move back up here, but I guess the man in the dollhouse won't let them out.

I believe this item might lose something in oral form. It seems better on the page—like Amanda's letters.

Speaking of whom, I still don't feel peaceful about developments on that front. I have had no correspondence from my pen pal, but Mr. Pate called to thank me. He has been to North Carolina once and says that this job is a dream come true. He is already making plans to move the family.

I must find a special going-away present for dear Amanda.

I just hope I haven't set in motion a disaster. My instincts tell me that things will turn out all right, and I suppose now I can only trust that they will.

February 14th

Marcia read something out loud to us at the table today about the vast differences in generations. Here's a part of it. "In our day grass was mowed, Coke was only a cold drink, pot was something you cooked in, and rock music was Grandma's lullaby."

I also heard something at the table that I wasn't supposed to hear, but I did. This was said to a seat mate in a low voice: "How are you feelin', fella?"

"Like the butt end of disaster, if you really wanna know."

February 15th

I lay in bed last night thinking about a television show I had watched during the evening. It was a Valentine's Day special on that famous (infamous?) couple Edward VIII and Wallis Simpson. Why do I never tire of the drama of the Windsors? Maybe because I suffered through the actual event at a time when I was young and vulnerable. I cried when I listened to King Edward's voice over the radio as he abdicated the rule of an empire for the woman he loved. It seemed earth-shaking and *so* romantic.

Did he get short-changed? I now think so. I have thought so since reading an article some years ago about café society in New York, describing a group of toadies who hung around the aging Duchess and made fun of the aging Duke.

She, with them, called him "the little man," and whispered and laughed about him when they were not ignoring him.

Oo-oo-ooh! How delicious it would have been to hear HRH telling her off, something like this:

"Now just a moment, Wallis. I have had *enough*. Enough of you and your useless cronies ridiculing me. Maybe I am not what I was, but I am the man you married. I did this at something of a cost, if you remember. I don't expect gratitude, but I expect—I demand—the civility to which I am entitled."

Whooo-eee! The "little man" would have been eight feet tall in my estimation if he had said those words, or something like them!

Later

Reading over my scathing treatise, I've decided I may have been too hard on the lady. There are those who think that, even though she was scheming and ambitious to a fault, she nevertheless found ways to fill "the little man's" days and made him relatively happy in a *haut monde* (if useless) lifestyle. Maybe I don't know enough about it to get so worked up. Watch it, Hattie.

February 16th

More from the Silly Verse Department:

A GOOD BUT WORN-OUT SENTIMENT

"Have a nice day"
They say and say

And say and say and *say!*
Isn't it time they searched around
And found another way
To end a purchase or a deal,
Or just to be polite?
Those words have done their duty.
Let's retire them tonight!

GENEALOGY

I surely hate to think that I'm
Descended from primordial slime!
Best, when all is said and done,
To go along with Genesis One.

Adam (with Eve) as first begetter?
That's not perfect, but it's better
Than to think the ocean's scum
Is where my lineage started from!

February 20th

Amanda phoned to tell me good-bye. She and her mother
are leaving right away. Oh, dear. I have a little parting gift
for her. I will have to mail it.

She tried to sound cheerful. "Daddy is already in High
Point, and he has found a house with a yard big enough for
Buster and Kitty. He sounded so happy over the phone that
Mama says I mustn't cry.... We'll be back to visit Mama's
sister and her family, and all my friends. I'll see you then."

*I told her I would look forward to her next visit and
to please write and tell me all about her new home.*

Her voice sounded like it was choking up. I told her I would look forward to her visit and to please write and tell me all about her new home. After promising to continue to be pen pals, we quickly said our good-byes.

February 24th

At breakfast this morning I was told that Christine Summers had died in the night of a heart attack.

I was stunned. It couldn't *be*. I had sat by her last night at this very table—she had sat in that chair.... She had on that Schrader Sport teal dress of hers that I liked so much.... She couldn't be gone—out of this world forever.... *Oh, no!*

I left my breakfast untouched and fled to my apartment. If I passed anyone on the way they must have thought I was in a trance.... Chris had had some heart trouble, but we all thought that her bypass operation had fixed it. How was I going to do without her?

I found I couldn't stay by myself. I dashed over to Marcia's cottage, behind The Home. She had loved Chris, too, and when I told her the news we fell on each other and wept. I know she was thinking, as I was: *It could be you next, or me....* That's the trouble with a place like this.

There was a little bit of comforting news later. Christine had rung her bell, and help had come, very caring help. She was not alone at the last, and she had not suffered long.

February 26th

The chapel was full for Christine's memorial service. It was plain from Chaplain Brewer's remarks that he had appreciated the brightness with which she had shone in our midst.

I was pleased about the hymn he chose for us to sing: "Joyful, Joyful, We Adore Thee," with its wonderful words that Henry Van Dyke set to Beethoven's exultant music. I had heard Chris say it was her favorite hymn, as it is mine.

> Melt the clouds of sin and sadness,
> Drive the dark of doubt away.
> Giver of immortal gladness
> Fill us with the light of day....

And then:

> Teach us how to love each other.
> Lift us to the joy divine.

And then:

> Mortals, join the happy chorus
> Which the morning stars began.
>
> Father-love is reigning o'er us.
> Brother-love binds man to man.
> Ever singing, march we onward:
> Victors in the midst of strife.
> Joyful music leads us sun-ward,
> In the triumph song of life.

Even though our voices were quavering, we sang those words with great fervor, as if we hoped Christine Summers could hear us.... Maybe she did.

Marcia came to my rooms with me after the service. We had tea and talked about Christine.

"Remember," said Marcia, "how hard she worked, with you, to get a better place for Arthur and his family to live?"

"'Deed I do. A lot of the credit for Kudzu Kottage should go to her—and the credit for a lot of other good things that she did quietly. Best of all, though, was her sense of humor.... I'm so glad we had fun together, that last night at supper...."

"Tell me about it. I could use a laugh, or even a smile."

"Well, let me see.... I think I started it by something I remembered: a Lum and Abner radio show from one December night, years ago. They were in the Jot 'Em Down Store. Abner asked Lum what he was going to give his wife for Christmas. Lum said, 'A pair of mules.' Abner, not being up on the names of ladies' bedroom slippers, thought that was a kind of strange gift for a young woman; but, not to be outdone, he went out in the country and bought his fiancée (what *was* her name??) a pair of mules, the long-eared, braying kind. Abner just couldn't understand why she didn't appreciate the gift.

"Christine came back with a memory of Amos 'n Andy—I forget exactly, now—something about the Kingfish and the lodge brothers. She was so good at imitating the Kingfish's deep, rolling syllables. We agreed that those shows had it all over today's so-called comedy shows on TV.... I remember Chris saying, 'And by agreeing to that, Hattie, we're showing our age. We're playing the Everything-

Was-Better-Back-Then record. But do you know something? Lots of things *were* better. I wish I could have taped all of them.'

"We all agreed with her, but 'Who had a tape recorder?' I asked. 'I don't remember seeing one until about thirty years ago.... It was at a dinner party,' I recalled to the group. 'One of the guests brought his new tape recorder and slipped it under the dinner table, unbeknownst to the rest of us. I remember that he stayed pretty quiet during the meal, while the rest of us chattered away. Then, later, in the living room, he played the tape for us.

"Oh, dear! We couldn't believe how we sounded. I was mortified. 'Those are my words, but that is *not* my voice,' I protested. 'Oh, yes it is, Hattie! That's exactly the way you sound.' What a blow! I could not believe that that silly, corny twang had come out of my mouth. I sounded like Miss Backwoods County. I decided to take a vow of silence.

"That really made Chris laugh," I recounted to Marcia, "the idea of me being silent. Then Chris told us about an embarrassing moment she had at a very elegant dinner party when she was about eighteen. She was more than a little nervous. (She hadn't been 'out' long.) At the end of the meal the butler passed gold-tipped cigarettes. She had never seen that kind before. Trying to look sophisticated, she took one and lit the wrong end! How we laughed over that!"

We sipped our tea and were quiet.

"I simply cannot yet believe that I will never laugh with her again.... I'll tell you something, Marcia. Sudden death is a blessing, sometimes; but there is also a cruelty about it.

Those who are left behind have had no time to prepare for the parting."

"I suppose so," she said, "if there's any way to prepare for such a sadness."

"Maybe we should adopt the Boy Scout motto: 'Be Prepared.' Oh, me. I don't want to prepare for such partings."

We decided to have a glass of wine and turn on the television. Maybe Oprah would have something we could grin over.

11

Fresh Starts

March 13th

I can't consider this Friday the thirteenth unlucky. It has produced two gifts.

First, Arthur Priest brought me a beautiful bunch of radishes from the garden. He said he and Dolly had planted the seeds with the children a few weeks ago. They chose radishes because they mature fast and always charm young, first-time gardeners.

The "first fruits" of early spring brightened my spirit. I have had a spell of sadness, Dear Diary, missing Christine, and Amanda as well, but the excitement of life is pushing its way into my soul, just as our lovely daffodils are pushing up their cheerful heads.

The second gift was a letter in Amanda's dear and familiar hand in my box today.

Dear Miss Hattie,

Thank you for mailing me that pretty forget-me-not pin. I love it. I will forget-you-not, I prommise!

I miss Drayton, but I like the hills here. They are more fun on a bike or skates. I need brakes.

The people here talk kind of funny and say some funny things. I keep looking at my heels to see if there is any tar on them yet.

Mama and Daddy are so happy that it makes me happy. Oh, and we had some SNOW last week! It was the first I've ever seen ecsept on TV. You should have seen Buster and Kitty playing in it. It didn't last long, but it was fun.

I miss you.

Love,
Amanda

It may have snowed on our neighbor to the north, the Tarheel State, but things have been fairly bursting around here lately. Spring is arriving in our Lowcountry, and no matter one's age, there *is* something energizing about this time of year. Azaleas are blooming along with the daffodils, and the birds have been singing up a storm.

Folks at The Home have been all a-twitter, too, with exciting news.

"Hattie!" Retta called out when I came into the lobby yesterday. "Have you heard?"

"Heard what?"

"Paul is one of the three finalists in the car-naming contest! He just had a phone call."

"How perfectly wonderful! That means he's bound to win one of the prizes. Is that right?"

"Right," she said. "He won't know until the broadcast announcement. They want him to be there, in New York, three weeks from Friday!"

"Where is he now?" I asked.

"I think he went to his room to catch his breath. We kind of stampeded him. Oh, Hattie—Isn't it something?"

"Fabulous. Hard to take in. For such a thing to happen at our staid old residence is unbelievable." I found myself shaking with excitement and wanting to find some way to shower congratulations on our smart contestant. (Not only is Paul smart, he's popular.)

I saw Cora standing to one side looking a little subdued.

"I'm glad *some*body can win something," she said, a trifle ruefully.

Retta suggested that we have a celebration at supper. She and Cora went to a place on the square in Drayton and bought balloons and flags and horns—all kinds of party stuff—not enough for everyone, but some for each table. I talked with Mr. Detwiler, who gave his blessing. Then I visited the chef, who promised some special goodies: ice cream, cake squares, and candles. Hazel, one of the cooks, was persuaded to turn out one of our favorite things: a large batch of her delicious cheese biscuits.

We all came to supper early and waited to surprise Paul—
but he didn't come! Maybe he was still recovering from the
shock. Anyway, Curtis finally had to go to Paul's room and
haul him out, looking a little bit disheveled and a lot surprised. We waved flags and blew horns, and tapped our
glasses with our knives, and sang "For He's a Jolly Good
Fellow." Paul blushed as he stammered his thanks. Somebody had hooked up the PA system, and he spoke into the
microphone.

"I'm overcome," he said. "Maybe this is good practice for
what is coming up in New York. But I'll tell you one thing:
no matter what kind of audience is there, it won't have the
same meaning for me that this audience does."

We stopped him to clap for that statement. Then he went
on. "That first Friday in April, at eight o'clock, I hope you
will all be in here looking at that." He pointed to the large
TV screen. "I'll try to pretend that I'm just talking to you-
all, and maybe I won't be so scared."

"Scared, Paul? *You?*" said Cecil, stepping up to the microphone. "You'll knock 'em dead. Anyway, you won't have to
say much but 'Thank you,' and then kiss the check. And by
the way—speaking of checks, of rewards—I seem to remember giving you...or, rather, *lending* you...several excellent car names. Did you just happen to send in one of
my suggestions?"

"No, I didn't, Cecil. I'm grateful to everybody here who
supplied me with good names, but the three I sent in all
came out of here." He touched his forehead.

"Shoot!" retorted Curtis. "I liked the one I gave him: Stallion."

There was much laughter and banter throughout supper, and there was a lot of teasing about what he could, or should, do with the money—everyone was certain he would win the *grand* prize.

Bill Nixon said, "Paul, you could go to Tahiti and lie under a banana tree for the rest of your life. When you get hungry, just reach up and pull."

"No, Bill," said somebody else. "That would get tiresome. I think he ought to rent a cabin on the QE II and just sail around the world—wherever that great ship goes—just sailing and seeing the world...and eating...and sleeping...."

"And missing us!" was someone's thought.

"Right," said Paul. "I'd miss this place too much. Maybe I've been here too long. I don't want to be anywhere else. Oh, I'm looking forward to three days in New York, but that will be enough."

The party began to break up, with much slapping of Paul's back. A few of the men stayed behind. I found out that they were getting up a pool of bets as to which of the prizes Paul would win!

Big doings! What with the Tales and Taradiddles Night coming up, too, I hope we can stand all the excitement.

March 16th

Paul asked me—begged me, really—to go to Charleston with him to help him pick out an outfit for his TV appearance.

"Being a widower," he said, "I've just let my wardrobe go.

I haven't bought a suit in ten or twelve years. Seems kind of extravagant to get a new one at my ancient age. Anyway, it won't just be worn in New York. I can be buried in it!"

We managed to slip out this morning without anyone seeing us. There's absolutely nothing between Paul and me except friendship; but we both know how a trip to Charleston—as a duo—might be construed by some of our imaginative fellow retirees.

We went to the best men's store in downtown Charleston. The clerk didn't seem to take much interest in his elderly customer until I took him aside and clued him in.

"National TV? In New York? Well, let's get this gentleman fixed up!"

And this he did, very nicely: a gray suit only slightly darker than Paul's hair, and of beautiful material. A pale gray shirt and a gorgeous maroon tie completed the elegant ensemble.

"As Cecil said, 'You'll knock 'em dead!'" I declared, as we left the store.

"Sure," he replied. "Tom Cruise, move over!"

We had lunch at a restaurant atop one of the "tall" buildings in Charleston (ten stories). We managed to get a table by the window, where we had a clear view of the gracious old city between its two rivers.

Paul said, "Hattie, I don't want you to look at the right-hand column on this menu. I don't care what this meal costs today. Get anything you want, and I will, too.... My father used to use an old-time expression. When he felt slightly 'flush' with money, he'd say, 'I've got cotton in Augusta!' I think that saying dates back a long time. There were huge cotton warehouses in Augusta, and if you could get your cotton down to one of those warehouses you had it made. Well, I don't have cotton in Augusta, but with one prize or another coming from National Motors, let's splurge!"

And we did! We had a memorable lunch: She-Crab Soup, Shrimp Scampi, wine, all kinds of goodies not generally on our menu at FairAcres.

Over coffee we talked about his upcoming trip.

"I haven't been to New York in years," said Paul.

"Excited?" I asked.

"A little," he said, and looked out of the window with a wistful expression. Paul has aged gracefully. His hair has turned a nice shade of silver—not salt-and-pepper. His ears lie flat, he has good teeth, and his eyes beam with a pleasing mixture of brightness and—what shall I call it?— empathy? Anyway, he looks at you as if he's really seeing you. He's not exactly handsome. He's something better.

"I wish I had a daughter," he said. "I'd take her with me. We'd see a play or two, and go to the Rainbow Room...."

"You never had any children?"

"We had one. A son. But Ellie had such a hard time delivering that she said, 'No more.'"

"Well, its good that you have a son, anyway." It occurred to me that I had never heard him mention an offspring.

"I suppose so. I hear that he's parting with his third wife. I seldom see him. He was his mama's boy from the first. I always wanted a daughter."

I couldn't help thinking: *What a fine father of a daughter you would have made: sympathetic, intuitive, fun-loving....*

"I've never heard you talk about your wife."

After a quiet minute he said, "I nursed her for the last four years of her life, Hattie. She was a complete invalid. For the life of me I couldn't help feeling relieved when she finally passed away—and then I was weighted down with guilt for feeling that way."

Poor man. "But there were some good years, weren't there?"

"I suppose so.... Ellie was an only child. Beautiful, but rather self-centered. Not very interested in my career. Maybe I was *too* interested in my career.... I found the advertising field completely fascinating."

"I can see how it would be challenging," I said. "You were competing for the world's attention."

"That's exactly what we were doing, Hattie. You put it well. Of course, a career in advertising is not as glamorous as many people think. It can be a kind of slavery: eighteen-hour days at times, fierce competition, boring compilations, many disappointments...many excitements, too. If I were younger I would like to be working for the ad firm that is handling this contest."

"I'll say this for 'em," I put in. "They have good taste!"

He grinned. "You don't know, yet. I don't even know which of my three names they picked. But I'll admit something to you, my friend. This has given me a wonderful lift. Even if I win third prize, it's a boon—it's like—well, it's like a dollop of icing on the cake, at the last part of my life!"

His eyes were shining. I smiled at him and thought, *Praise God for the National Motors Corporation.*

Since it was only two o'clock we decided to extend our spree by going to the Battery. We stood on its wall and gazed out at Fort Sumter, where the "Late Unpleasantness" started. It was while we were standing there, caught up in ancient history, that we heard a horn blowing and a chorus of "Hi, Paul!" and "Hi, Hattie!"

When we turned, startled out of our reverie, we saw a stretch limousine, which had stopped and was holding up traffic while its occupants waved and yelled at us. Then I remembered: It was Louly Canfield's birthday. Having no children to honor her, she had decided to honor herself. She had hired a limo and driver to come to Drayton to pick up her and some friends for a gala day.

Oh, dear! We're in for it now, I thought. I could already imagine the reports of our sighting circulating through the residents.

We waved at them, and they soon moved on, beaming and twittering and waving handkerchiefs gaily. It was plain to see that they were having a wonderful day.

Later

I went to Louly's room tonight to tell her why Paul and I happened to be in Charleston together. I begged her not to make anything of what she had seen today.

To my surprise, she seemed to understand completely. She promised to pass on to her friends my hope that nothing "untoward" would be made of what was only a shopping trip.

"I hope your feelings weren't hurt that I didn't include you today, Hattie."

Oh dear! We're in for it now, *I thought.*

"Heavens, no! It hadn't even occurred to me to feel hurt!"
I assured her.

"You see," said Louly, "you have your children who come
to see you and take you out. I picked four people who have
no one—who never get asked out."

"I think that was *so* thoughtful of you, Louly. You all
looked like you were having great fun."

"Oh, we were! We stopped at the Old Market and bought
some interesting things. We even went to Saks Fifth Avenue! I didn't know there was a Saks in Charleston. We
didn't buy anything there, but it was fun to look. We had a
delicious lunch at the Mills House with wine and lemon
mousse and lots of other wicked and delicious things. Then
we went across that up-and-down bridge to Mt. Pleasant.
We saw the ocean, and then we came home along the Mark
Clark Expressway. In a stretch limo! Ooh, it was lovely! My
budget is shot, but it will recover. That limo! Honey, we felt
like the chauffeur was half a block away! I shall live on this
day for a long time."

Louly's eyes were shining. What a great idea she had had.

March 17th

So far there has apparently been no gossiping. I can't quite
believe it, but I'm gratified.

After lunch I "retired" to my quarters and searched my
memory, trying to decide what kind of tale or taradiddle
I could produce for our "do."

My mind went all the way back to my twelfth year, when
my mother decided that elocution lessons would be good

for my self-confidence, and my "social presence." (Oh, dear!) Would there be anything in that experience I could use?

There was at that time in my hometown a woman who was a frustrated actress. She had never made it in the theatrical world, and I am now sure why. She over-emoted. Later in life she made her living teaching young people to over-emote.

I am glad there are no home videos of her elocution recitals. I would die if I thought my children would ever see me "elocuting" in the high-flown vignettes and poems she taught us.

I recited one pretentious poem (before a large audience, I now remember with a shudder) called "Curfew Shall Not Ring Tonight!" I have almost forgotten the highly dramatic story portrayed in those verses. I believe it was about a girl whose lover was slated to be executed (for some crime or other that he did not commit) when the curfew bell rang on a certain evening.

The girl couldn't stand it. She climbed the tall bell tower, vowing that the curfew bell would not ring that night. As the ringing was about to start she grabbed the bell's rope, and, with the weight of her body, kept the clapper from hitting the bell.

I remember only one stanza, which I will put down, complete with the gestures I used:

Out she swung. Far out.
(I swept my right arm forward)

The city seemed a speck of light, below.
(I looked down, shading eyes with hand)
There, twixt Heaven *(I pointed upward)*
and Earth *(I pointed downward)* suspended,
As the bell swung to *(arm to the right)*
and fro. *(arm to the left)*

How could my mother have put me through that?... No, I think I will have to find something else to do for my tale. I don't want to go through those ridiculous motions again, even though I'm sure they would get a laugh. They didn't get a laugh at age twelve, nor were they supposed to. It's just too embarrassing a memory, from a painful time of life.

March 18th

I had another letter from High Point today—but not from Amanda this time. From her father.

> *Dear Mrs. McNair,*
> *I should have written to you sooner to thank you for what you have done for my family and me. We have been real busy getting settled in a new home, and I have been busy learning the furniture business.*
> *There is a lot to learn, but since it is a field I like above all else, I am enjoying going to work every day. It is good when you can see beautiful results.*
> *Amanda has been a little homesick, but I think she will feel better when she makes some friends (which, thankfully, she does very easily).*

*I hope all goes well with you. I will never forget
your kindness to me, or the kindness of your friend
Mrs. Metcalf.*

Yours gratefully,
Terry Pate

Isn't that a nice letter, Dear Diary? I'm going to save it,
and from now on, if any people get after me for being a
busybody, I will just wave that letter in their faces.

12

Close Calls

March 20th

Guess what, Dear Diary? There's a sequel to the "Purloined Portrait" story!

The culprits and I had thought that the painting would not be discovered until after the three of us "in the know" were long gone. But no! Fate has deemed otherwise.

Today's copy of our newspaper, *Family Affairs,* carried the following article:

> Mr. Jonathan Guthrie has written us that he plans to come to FairAcres Home next week with the purpose of carrying out the wishes of his mother, the late Suzannah Guthrie, who generously bequeathed to us the money for the erecting of our beautiful chapel.

Mr. Guthrie says, "My mother preferred that a church's choir be located in the back of the sanctuary. She felt strongly that the beauty of the music was what was important, not the looks of the choir members. I have always regretted that funds gave out before we could complete the rear portion of the building as she wanted it. I am now able to supply the funds to do this."

Oh, dear! My hands shook a little as I folded the paper.... The portrait will be found. I know that. I just pray that the identities of the two who hid it can somehow, miraculously, remain undiscovered.

March 25th

The news went through The Home like wildfire today. Ole Pukey Face had come to light again! We groaned to each other as word spread.

There was much speculation as to how the portrait had reached its hiding place. I think the secret will die with the three of us.

What concerns us even more is, will it be rehung in the dining room? It is now in an art shop having its damaged frame repaired.

A delegation formed to approach Mr. Detwiler again. Poor man. He's being "delegated" to death. They asked if Mr. Nelson Purifoy could be persuaded to hang the portrait in The Home's office.

"Oh, you want *me* to have the pleasure of his company,"